The Black Book
[DIARY OF A TEENAGE STUD]
VOL. II

Stop, Don't Stop

JONAH BLACK

AVON BOOKS
An Imprint of HarperCollins Publishers

The Black Book [Diary of a Teenage Stud], Vol. II:
Stop, Don't Stop

Copyright © 2001 by 17th Street Productions,
an Alloy Online, Inc. company.

Cover photograph from Tony Stone
Design by Russell Gordon

Printed in the United States of America.

For information address
HarperCollins Children's Books, a division of
HarperCollins Publishers, 1350 Avenue of the Americas,
New York, NY 10019.

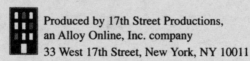 Produced by 17th Street Productions,
an Alloy Online, Inc. company
33 West 17th Street, New York, NY 10011

Library of Congress Catalog Card Number: 2001116875
ISBN 0-06-440799-3

First Avon edition, 2001

AVON TRADEMARK REG. U.S. PAT. OFF.
AND IN OTHER COUNTRIES,
MARCA REGISTRADA, HECHO EN U.S.A.

Visit us on the World Wide Web!
www.harperteen.com

— ■ —

Stop, Don't Stop

— ■ —

Oct. 19, 3:35 P.M.

Sophie puts her hand on my cheek and says, "Jonah? Are you awake?"

I open my eyes and there she is, her cheeks still red from the wind on the Maine seacoast. She is wearing a yellow slicker over white canvas overalls and giant black rubber boots and a yellow rain hat. *Are we going fishing?* I wonder.

"It's seven A.M.," she whispers. "Don't you want to wake up?"

I sit up in bed. Her pajamas are folded on the pillow. "Sophie," I say, yawning. "What time is it?"

"It's the best time of the day," she says. "Come on; they're biting."

"Who's biting?" I say.

"You'll see," she tells me mysteriously.

—— ∎ ——

She opens the door and leaves the room, and I quickly pull my clothes on and run after her. Sophie is down by the shore with all this fishing gear in the sand, and she casts her line into the wild surf. The sun is rising over the ocean, turning the sky crimson and pink.

"What are we trying to catch?" I ask her.

Sophie smiles at me, and her smile is the brightest, most wonderful thing I have ever seen. *I'm going to remember this forever,* I think.

Then the line goes tight and the reel starts whizzing and spinning around. Sophie tries to get control of the rod, but whatever is on her line is way too big.

"Whoa," she says. "It's enormous."

"What is it?" I say. "Sophie, what did you catch?"

For just a second we link eyes, and there is something desperate and hungry in her gaze. "Jonah," Sophie says, still struggling with the rod. "I'm afraid."

Before I can help her, Sophie is lifted off of her feet and hurled into the ocean, and a second later she's gone without a trace. The waves crash on the beach in front of me.

"Sophie?" I shout, but my voice is blown away by the fierce wind. "Sophie?"

I plunge into the ocean, but there's no sign of

her. I can feel the shells beneath my bare feet. I'm in up to my neck.

"Sophie?"

In front of me a giant fluke flashes silvery in the water, like the tail of a mermaid. It arcs above the surface, and a second later it's gone. I'm not even certain it really happened. Maybe it was a mirage.

I remain standing in the cold Atlantic, calling out Sophie's name, over and over, but I've lost her.

Suddenly a woman's head and shoulders emerge from the waves. Her hair is wet, and she isn't wearing a shirt. For a moment I think it's Sophie and start to swim over to her, but then I realize it's not her.

"Posie?" I say. "What are you doing here?"

Posie looks frightened, and then she dives beneath the waves. Now there's no sign of either of them, so I dive beneath the surface as the next wave crashes over my head and everything is dark and cold and I can't see anything. It's quiet down here, and the world seems very far away.

I try to call Posie's name, but my voice doesn't carry underwater.

And a voice said, "Don't try to talk."

There was a crack in the darkness and all I could think was, *This is what a chicken sees when it comes out of its shell*. So I kind of moved toward the crack and then more light shone in, and my head started pounding like my brain was too big for my skull.

"Jonah?" she said. "Can you see me?"

I looked at her but she didn't look anything like Posie.

"I'm Dr. Sheldon. Do you know where you are?" the woman said.

I looked around. Things were very bright and white.

"Am I underwater?" I said.

Dr. Sheldon smiled. "Jonah, you're in the hospital. You had an accident during the diving meet. Do you remember diving?" she asked me.

Then I remembered. "I was on the high dive," I whispered.

"That's right," she said gently.

"A back two-and-a-half somersault," I said.

"Yes." She nodded.

"With . . . a one-and-a-half twist."

Dr. Sheldon smiled. She bent over me and touched the side of my cheek with her hand. She looked very young for a doctor. She had on a black turtleneck and a white coat, and a stethoscope was swinging from her neck like a big necklace. She strokes my hair and says, *I love you, Jonah Black. I love you more than I have ever loved a patient.* I look into her eyes and I realize it's Posie, after all. What's she doing, pretending she's a doctor?

Posie crawls into the bed with me and she

reaches over and touches the automatic bed adjustment button with her strong tan fingers, and the head of the bed slowly tilts back. I can feel her lips on my throat, and she says, *I've cured you, Jonah. Thank heavens you're cured at last.*

"I'm cured," I said, and opened my eyes. Dr. Sheldon was still standing over me, but she was wearing a different outfit now. It must have been hours later.

"I'm glad you're up again," she said. "Do you remember where you are?"

"Some hospital," I said. I looked around. "Where's Posie?"

"Posie?" Dr. Sheldon said, and smiled. "I'm not sure which one she is."

"Which one?" I said, confused.

"You have a lot of fans, Jonah. There have been quite a few young ladies here to see you."

I realized as she said this that I was lying there with my bare butt sticking out of my hospital gown, and there was a wet spot on the pillow where I'd been drooling. I'm sure I looked fantastic. I hope Posie didn't see me that way.

Then I started wondering who else would come to see me? Luna Hayes? Or maybe Watches Boys Dive, that Indian girl who I keep seeing in the bleachers during diving practice?

"Who . . ." I said, but my voice sounded like mush.

"You hit your head on the diving board. During the swim meet," the doctor said. "Do you remember?"

"Yeah," I said. I remembered how in the middle of the dive I'd lost my concentration because I was thinking about Sophie and Posie and what I was going to do about them. I was trying to choose between them, between the girl of my dreams and my real-life friend. And the choice seemed so obvious. It was Posie I should be with. *I'm completely in love with Posie,* I realized. Then I whacked my head on the board.

"You've experienced a major ligamental strain of the cervical area. You're going to have a stiff neck. I want you to wear a clamshell collar for now," Dr. Sheldon said.

"A clamshell collar?" I said.

"Yes. And I'm giving you Flexeril for muscle spasms, ibuprofen as an anti-inflammatory, and Lorcet for pain," she said.

"Will I be able to dive again?" I said.

"Not for a while, Jonah. I want you to rest your neck," the doctor said.

"But I'm going to miss the season!" I said.

"Let's see how well you recover. You didn't do any major damage. But don't be surprised if you experience some nausea, blurry vision, photophobia, or dizziness. You'll probably also feel a little spacey for the next week or so. Do you feel spacey, Jonah?" she asked me.

I look out the window, and Posie sails across the bright blue sky on her surfboard. She waves to me.

"A little," I said.

"You're a very lucky boy, Jonah," the doctor said.

"Yes," I said, closing my eyes.

"Jonah?" I opened my eyes, and a nurse was standing there. It must have been later again. I had no idea how much time had passed.

"Huh?" I said sleepily.

"You have some visitors. Do you feel up to seeing people?" she asked me.

"Yes," I said. "Definitely. Who is it?"

"It's your big sister and your mother," the nurse said.

"Little," I said.

The nurse frowned worriedly. "Little what?"

"Little sister. She only looks older. She skipped a . . . skipped a . . ." I suddenly felt so exhausted I couldn't go on explaining what I was trying to explain.

"She skipped a grade? Your little sister skipped a grade?" the nurse said.

I nodded, desperately wishing I could go back to

sleep. Remembering how I'd been forced to repeat my junior year, while my little sister was now a senior, made me feel extremely tired.

"I'll tell them not to stay too long," the nurse said kindly. Then she showed my mother and my sister, Honey, into the room. My mother had tears running down her cheeks and she threw herself at me and crushed me with a giant hug. I felt like she was going to snap me in two.

"My baby!"

"Hey, Flounder Nuts," said my sister. "They've got you in one of those collars."

"Yeah," I said.

"Jonah," said my mother. "The doctor told us you might be a little out of it. Are you out of it, sweetie?"

"A little," I admitted.

"Ma," said Honey. "Look at him. He's high as a kite."

"I am not," I said. Actually though, the walls *were* kind of breathing in and out. Is that normal? I can't seem to remember what is normal anymore and what is not.

"I flew back as soon as I heard you'd been injured," my mother said dramatically.

"Flew back?" I said.

"Yes, don't you remember, darling? I'm in the

middle of the media tour for my book. *Hello Penis! Hello Vagina!* Remember my book, Jonah? It tells young people all about their bodies. It's called *Hello Penis! Hello Vagina!* Do you remember my book, *Hello Pe—*"

"I remember it, Mom." Although I honestly wished I didn't.

"Oh, good," said Mom. "I'm so glad!"

"Mom was in Pittsburgh," Honey said.

"You didn't have to interrupt your tour, Mom. I'm all right." I said, but then I remembered how disappointed I'd been that she wasn't in the audience at the diving meet.

"Bup, bup, bup," Mom said, holding her hand out to indicate that I shouldn't say anything more. "The minute I heard you were hurt I took the next plane back. My baby! I've been so worried about you!" She looked at her watch.

"Mom's flying back to Pittsburgh this afternoon," Honey told me.

"You are?" I said, feeling kind of hurt. I mean, Mom stopped her tour for one day to make sure I was still alive, and now she was taking off again? Typical. Never mind the fact that her book and her radio show are like, a complete joke, because she's pretending to be this doctor with degrees in psychology and teen sexuality and whatever, but she barely even finished college! She told me herself her grades were never very good, which is one of the reasons she's so proud of me and Honey. We're good students. At least, I used to be.

I wish I had a normal mother. I wish I had a normal sister. I wish my father acted like he had the slightest interest what time zone me and my sister live in. I wish a lot of things, actually. I guess I'm just feeling a little sorry for myself. Forget it.

"Well," Mom said. "Now that I know you're all right. You are all right, aren't you?"

"Yeah. I'm great." I tried to sound bitter and ironic, but Mom didn't pick up on it.

"Good," she said. She bent down and crushed me again with a giant hug.

"Ow!"

"Mom, don't squeeze him like that," Honey hissed. "Jesus."

"I'm glad you're all right," Mom said, heading toward the door. "I'm very glad. You've got my cell phone number, right? Okay, 'bye!" She blew me a kiss and then practically ran out the door.

Honey watched her leave, then looked at me.

"You're really okay?" she said. I was kind of touched that Honey seemed to really care how I was doing. Expressing tenderness for her only sibling is not exactly Honey's strong suit.

"Uh-huh," I said. "I'm pretty out of it, though."

"That was some dive you did. You should have seen everybody screaming when you fell into the water. It was pretty goddamned dramatic," she said. She sounded really impressed.

Impressing Honey wasn't quite what I'd intended.

"God, I can't believe I did that," I muttered.

Honey got out a cigarette, stuck it in her mouth, and lit it. Next to her was a big sign that said: DANGER: OXYGEN.

"Believe it," she said.

Honey walked to the door and paused. "I'm glad you're all right, you bastard. You do that again and I'll kill you myself," she said. Then she left.

I lay there in the hospital bed with my neck in the clamshell collar and closed my eyes. From outside I could hear the sound of the surf crashing against the public beach in town. Pompano Beach, Florida. What a strange place to grow up. With the surfers out on the water, and the tourists on the Mile, and the millionaires on their yachts cruising up the Intercoastal Waterway, and Don Shula High School, and the softly blowing palm trees, and the tan girls in bikinis everywhere. Posie always wears a bikini. She's a surfing queen.

I opened my eyes and sat up and looked out the hospital window. I couldn't see the ocean and I couldn't see Posie anymore.

11

Oct. 20, 10:30 A.M.

Good news! The doctor says I can go home soon, like maybe tomorrow. They still have me on all these drugs, though, and they make me really spacey. In a way I'm glad I was asleep when all those girls visited me, because if I'd been awake I would have definitely made a fool of myself.

But I do feel like talking to someone. Like Thorne or Posie. I could even call Sophie up in Maine. I still have her number. But what would be the point? I'd say who I was and Sophie would say, "Jonah? Jonah *Who*? Do I know you?"

And then I'd have to explain how I went to Masthead Academy with her, I'm the guy that got kicked out. And now I'm back here in Pompano Beach, repeating eleventh grade because Masthead wouldn't give me my credits, and all my friends are seniors now. And I'd say, "I guess I was wondering if you knew the reason I got thrown out was because of you?"

And she'd say, "Who is this really?"

And I'd say, "Forget it; I'm not anybody you would remember."

And then she'd hang up.

(Still Oct. 20, 4:45 P.M.)

I nodded off this afternoon, and when I woke up a girl was sitting down in a chair next to my bed, watching me. It was Cecily LaChoy from German class. She was reading *YM* and chewing gum. I couldn't believe it. I mean, why would Cecily come and see me? I hardly know her. I met her one time at the party at Luna Hayes's house a couple of weeks ago, but that's it. I mean, the odds of Cecily LaChoy visiting me in the hospital are about the same as getting a phone call from Madonna.

The nurse came in and asked, "Has he woken up yet?" and Cecily said no.

I lay there with my eyes closed, not sure if I was supposed to be awake or not. "He looks cute asleep, doesn't he?" said the nurse.

"He does," said Cecily. "Like a little boy."

"He's going to be all right," the nurse said. "He didn't bruise his brain. That's the main risk in a case like this."

"You can do that?" Cecily said. "Bruise your brain?"

"Some people. But not Jonah here. He just got a little smack and lost consciousness for a while. It could have been much worse. We're sending him home tomorrow."

Cecily got up and said, "Don't tell him I was here," and then I heard the sound of her leaving and the nurse shuffling around the room, and then the door closed. The room was full of this lavender smell that must have been from Cecily's shampoo. Cecily is definitely pretty in her own way. I never really thought much about her before.

When I opened my eyes there was a long-stemmed red rose next to the bed. Next to it was a card that read: *For Jonah. With love, A Friend.*

I picked up the rose and smelled it. Falling on my head might be the best thing that's ever happened to me.

Thorne was here this morning. Dr. Sheldon said I could take off the clamshell collar. So the first thing Thorne did when he came here is ask if he could borrow it. He thinks it's a chick magnet.

"It's unbelievable," he said. "All the girls at school think you're like this little wounded bird. They all want to take care of you, man. I've never seen anything like it. I want to know where they sell those collars. I could make a fortune on those."

I thought about telling him about Cecily coming to the hospital and leaving me the rose, but I decided not to.

Thorne had gotten sunburned since I last saw him. He was sitting in the chair next to my bed, wearing a yellow T-shirt and a pair of black shorts.

He had an earring in his left ear, and I suddenly recognized this earring. It was one of Posie's, a golden seashell.

"Hey, Thorne, where'd you get the sunburn? Were you out surfing?" I asked. I could imagine Posie teaching him how to surf.

Thorne's eyes were kind of shifting from side to side like he was nervous or something. "Nah. I got this on the boat," he said.

"Which boat?" I remembered him telling me something about his father's new boat but I couldn't remember what he'd said.

"My pop's sailboat. I'm working for him on weekends. It's awesome. A sloop. It's the best, man. Tourists line up around the block in Lauderdale just to take a sunset cruise," he said. "We're raking it in."

"That sounds great," I said.

"It's hardly like working, I'm telling you. It's like lying around on a sailboat twanging thong bikinis," Thorne said.

I laughed. "Wow, I'd love to come with you sometime. You think I could?"

Thorne shook his head. "I don't know," he said. "Have to check it out with the old man. He's pretty stingy. Doesn't want anyone on board unless they're a paying customer."

"Well maybe I could like, help out some weekend? I wouldn't mind working if I could go out on the boat," I offered.

Thorne looked out the window. "I'll ask him about it, okay?"

"Okay," I said.

Thorne kept looking out the window, and we didn't talk for a while.

"So how's school?" I asked.

"Creepy," Thorne said. "Mr. Bond has been acting all zippy this week. I think he's finally getting some."

"Oh, man. There are some things I don't want to know," I said. Mr. Bond is the senior class homeroom teacher. That's the only good thing about being held back. My homeroom teacher, Miss von Esse, has a much prettier face.

Thorne looked at his watch. "Hey, Jonah, can you hang on a second?"

This made me laugh. I was in a hospital bed; where did he think I was going? I nodded.

Thorne got out his cell phone and punched in a number. "Hey, Kendra. It's me. What's up? Uh-huh. That's what I thought."

He sat there listening to this Kendra person for a second. I didn't know who Kendra was.

"I agree," he said. "So let's sell those suckers.

17

Yeah. Sell all of 'em. Put it into treasuries. Fine. Okay. Later."

He hung up and grinned at me.

"Let me guess," I said. "She's your personal broker?"

"Oh, yeah," Thorne said. "It doesn't get more personal than Kendra."

Thorne laughed, and I laughed, and while we were laughing, I was like, I have absolutely no idea what we're laughing about. Thorne is always saying these smooth-sounding things, things that sound like they mean something, but the more you think about it, the less you really get it.

Thorne made another call. "Hi, Sally, it's me. How many you got for this week? Whoa! Excellent! Wait, let me write this down." He pulled a PalmPilot out of his pocket and started scribbling away with his little pen. "Okay, that's fourteen 'women looking for men,' twenty-eight 'men looking for women'—wow! Nine 'women alternative,' ten 'men alternative,' and two 'double dating.' Fantastic. How's the copy? Everything legal? Okay, let's put 'em on the Web. Yeah. No, I'm here seeing my friend Jonah. He's in the hospital. Oh, nothing serious. I'll see you later. 'Bye."

Thorne put away his cell phone and his PalmPilot. "All-time high number of personals in the Wood Love Connection Rendezvous. They just phone in the ads and put it on a credit card, I stick 'em up on the Web, and the next thing you know, everybody's making out. The wonders of technology, Jonah my man!" he shouted.

"How much do you make off of each of those ads?" I asked. It's funny; I have no idea what sort of money Thorne makes from all his scams. He always acts like he's this kid millionaire.

"Enough," he said. "Anyway. Are you okay with me and the Hoffster going out? I wanted to make sure you're all right with it, so it doesn't get, you know, weird."

"I don't care if you and Posie go out," I said. It was a huge lie, but I didn't know how to tell him that I think the fact that he and Posie are going out completely *sucks*.

"I don't believe you," Thorne said. "I think you're totally pissed off."

"Shut up," I said.

"I know you like her," Thorne said. "The only reason you haven't jumped her yourself is because you're still all into that chick up north. Sophie O'Brien. Did you call her yet?"

I hate it when your friends know you better than you know yourself sometimes.

"No," I said.

"Are you going to?" he said.

"I don't know."

Thorne shook his head. "I don't know about you, man. Here you've got all the chicks in the high school throwing themselves at you and it's like it doesn't make any difference to you. I mean, you could have sex with almost anybody now. You could like, send around a sign-up sheet."

"I don't want to have sex with anybody. I want it to mean something," I said quietly.

"I know, I know. You want to be *in love*. It's incredible. It's like you're something out of that Charles Dick," Thorne said.

I thought about this for a second.

"You mean Dickens? Charles Dickens?" I asked him.

"Yeah, whatever," he said.

A nurse came in and looked at Thorne and me like we were doing something illegal. "Jonah's going to need some rest soon," she told Thorne.

"I'm on my way out, miss," said Thorne, and then he smiled at her with his big Thorne teeth, and the nurse actually blushed.

Why do women buy his horseshit? Don't they know how full of it he is? Or maybe they do know, but they think he's charming anyway.

"Listen, Jonah," Thorne said, as the nurse

headed down the hall. "Remember when I found Sophie O'Brien's phone number and address for you off the Net? Remember the condition?"

"What condition?" I said.

"You said if I gave it to you, you'd finally tell me what happened with her. Why they threw you out of that fancy prep school and made you come back down here. You said you'd tell me the whole story about the—"

"The situation," I said. That's what all my teachers have been calling it.

"Yeah, whatever you want to call it. You said you'd tell me," Thorne said.

"I remember," I said.

Thorne scratched his goatee. It still hadn't grown in all the way.

"So?" he said.

"Okay, okay," I said impatiently. "I'll tell you. Maybe not this second, but I'll tell you." It kind of annoyed me that he wanted to have this whole big conversation right then while I was lying in the hospital.

"I didn't mean this second," Thorne said.

"I promise I will," I told him, even though I couldn't really imagine talking about it. I hadn't told anybody the whole story yet.

"You know I don't care what happened, right? There's nothing you could have done that was like, so perverted or demented, or whatever that I wouldn't forgive you," Thorne said. It was really big of him.

"Thanks, Thorne," I said, smiling. "I'll tell you sometime. I promise."

"All right," Thorne said.

He stood up and held the clamshell collar to his neck. "Oh, man. This is excellent. The girls are going to love this."

"Thorne?" I said. "If you're going out with Posie now, what do you need the collar for?"

Thorne looked at me for a second; then he threw his head back and laughed.

"Hoo boy," he said. "You almost had me going there for a second. Man, Jonah. You crack me up!"

He snapped on the collar. "So how do I look?"

I nodded. "Pathetic," I said.

"Excellent," Thorne said, looking very pleased with himself.

As he got up to go he said, "Okay, so don't forget to call that girl up north. That Sophie, okay? You got a date with destiny, Jonah."

He gave me the thumbs-up sign, and I gave him the thumbs-up sign, too, as he headed out.

But I'm *not* going to call Sophie. I don't want to talk to her anymore. The person I want to talk to is Posie. Where is she? How come she hasn't visited me? I wish she was mine.

It must be the middle of the night. I have a roommate here in the hospital now, and he snores like a lumber mill. His name is Gary Wilkinson and he just had his appendix out. How they even found his appendix is a mystery to me because this kid, who is probably about sixteen, is the size of a Volkswagen Beetle. I mean, he's the biggest kid I've ever seen. Underneath the blankets his body looks like an iceberg.

The drugs they have me on are really intense, like I can hear things that aren't even there. I think they've upped the dosages or something, because everything is just so jiggy, or something. Anyway, I'm awake now and I don't even know what time it is because the clock on the wall is broken. For all I know I could've been in a coma for twenty years and just woken up. Maybe I'm an old man now, except I just looked at my hand and it doesn't look wrinkled or anything.

I just had this dream that I was back at Masthead Academy. In the dream it's the morning before the formal dance and everything is frozen. I walk around the school, and it's like the whole world has stopped, like a video on Pause. I am the

23

only person moving. I walk over to Sullivan the Giant's desk and there are the folders he got from his father, full of dirt on every girl in the school. I go outside and there is the flag on the flagpole frozen in the icy wind. I go over to the girls' dorm and there is Sophie, sitting at her window, like a statue. I call out her name but she doesn't move. There is a tear halfway down her cheek, just stuck there. I walk over and touch it but it isn't wet. It's cold and frozen, too, like an icicle. Her fingernails have dark-purple polish on them.

I go outside thinking, *Now's my chance. I can fix everything before the dance even starts.* But I can't do anything because everything is stuck.

Suddenly Posie is there, wearing a wet suit for surfing, and she's running across the campus, the only moving thing in this entire frozen universe.

"Posie!" I call out. "Help me!"

But Posie just runs past me like I'm not even there, and she jumps into Thorne's VW Beetle and the two of them drive off toward Florida together, and I realize that as far as Posie's concerned, I'm just one more frozen person in this frozen place.

The clock hasn't even moved. The nurse just came in and put her hand on my forehead and said, "What are you doing awake, Jonah?"

And I said, "Am I awake? I'm sorry."

She made a *tsk* sound and then she checked my IV bag and said, "I think I'm going to ask the doctor to increase your painkillers."

Oct. 22, 7 A.M. (maybe)

Okay, so I realize my last entry made no sense. It looks like they've got my painkillers down now; in fact, I'm off the IV bag and I think I can go home today. Last night was pretty intense, though. I had some dreams or hallucinations or whatever that were even weirder than the one I wrote down. I'm not even sure I want to think about them.

When I woke up this morning, there was another rose on my pillow. Cecily LaChoy again?

I'm beginning to think Thorne is right about being pathetic. Girls love it.

Still no visit from Posie, though. I keep wondering where she is. I hope she's okay. It's weird not to hear from her. Actually, this is ridiculous. I'm calling her right now.

Okay, so I just got off the phone with Posie. It was great to hear her voice. I could practically smell the ocean in her hair just from being on the phone with her.

"Jonah, is that you? Hold on," she said kind of groggily. Then she fumbled with the phone. I guess I woke her up. "Are you okay?"

"Yeah, I'm okay. I should be home later on today," I said.

"Did the nurses tell you I came by?" Posie asked me.

What?!? I can't believe those stupid nurses! I can't believe Posie was here, and they never told me!

"Oh, no, they didn't tell you, did they?" Posie said. "You must feel totally neglected."

"It's all right," I said. "I've been kind of out of it anyway."

"You don't know how worried I've been!" Posie said. "Are you really all right?"

"I'm fine," I said. Hearing Posie say she was worried about me made me feel one hundred percent better. I think it cured me.

"What time is it?" Posie said, yawning.

"I think it's almost eight," I told her, although I really wasn't sure.

"Wait a second, let me check my—Whoa! It's six-fifteen!" she said.

"You're kidding, I'm sorry. I guess I kind of lost track of time in here. You go back to sleep," I told her.

"Jonah, it totally sucks that you're in the hospital. And it sucks even more that I haven't come to see you while you're awake. I'm going to make it up to you, though. I'm serious. Promise you're not mad at me?" Posie said.

"I promise," I said. I'm never mad at Posie for long.

"You could stop by today," I said. It sounded really pathetic, like I was begging her. "If you want to, I mean."

"Dammit, Jonah, I'd like to, but I've got surf practice. With the squad, you know? There's a big triple-A competition coming up, and I'm supposed to kick all those other girls' butts."

"How about afterward? I'll be home by then. You could come by my house."

"Well . . ." She sounded embarrassed. "Me and Thorne are grabbing some dinner, I think."

"Okay, whatever. Tell me about the weekend. You got any wild plans?" I asked her.

———— ■ ————

"Not really. Me and Thorne are going to go to the mall to check out the surf shop," she said.

"Right," I said. All I could think was, I'm never going to see her again. It's going to be Thorne this and Thorne that until I'm ninety-five years old.

"Are you okay with this?" Posie said. "With me and Thorne, I mean?" She paused. "I mean, the three of us have been best friends since like, the Civil War. I don't want Thorne and me going out to make you feel all, you know, left out, or anything. . . ."

The nurse came into my room with a tray of pills. She glared at me.

"Uh-oh. I gotta go, Posie," I said.

"Wait," Posie said. "You have to tell me if you're okay with me and Thorne being together."

I didn't know what to tell her. It wasn't okay. My head hurt.

"Don't worry," I said.

"Jonah," said the nurse.

"I gotta go," I told Posie.

"Okay," Posie said. "I'm going back to sleep. Just remember though, rock hard, okay?"

"Okay," I said.

"Say it, Jonah," Posie ordered.

"Rock hard," I said.

"Right," Posie said.

"You think you're gonna come by and visit?" I asked her.

"I don't know, Jonah. I'll try. Okay? See ya," she said.

"See ya."

I hung up. *Rock hard?* That's totally something Thorne would say, not Posie. So is Posie going to start acting like Thorne? He is going to ruin her, I can see it all now. Ouch. Just thinking that makes my heart hurt.

The doctor just came in. "I think I'm going to keep you here one more night," she said. "You need more rest."

"Fine," I said. All of a sudden I don't care so much about going home.

Oct. 23

I'm home. Honey picked me up in her Jeep and drove me back to the house, and now I'm lying on my bed. Out my sliding glass door I can see Honey sitting on a lounge chair, filling out some college applications and letting her toenails dry. She's painted them black.

AMERICA ONLINE INSTANT MESSAGE
FROM NORTHGIRL999, 10-23, 5:35 P.M.

NORTHGIRL999: Hello Jonah Black!
JBLACK94710: Aine! How are you? It's been a while since I heard from you.
NORTHGIRL999: I had midterm exams here at University of Stokholm. How are you?

<u>JBLACK94710:</u> Not so good. I injured myself during a diving meet last week. Hit my head on the board as I came down. I wound up in the hospital.

<u>NORTHGIRL999:</u> Oh poor diving board boy! Are you going to be fine?

<u>JBLACK94710:</u> Yeah. I didn't bruise my brain. It could have been a lot worse.

<u>NORTHGIRL999:</u> I am so glad you are all right!

<u>JBLACK94710:</u> Well I'm out for the season now. At least for the next couple of months.

<u>NORTHGIRL999:</u> Now you can work on studies. And girls! :)

<u>JBLACK94710:</u> Well, school is pretty easy for me this year. When I left Masthead Academy I got held back a year. So I'm back in 11th grade again. I had all these subjects last year.

<u>NORTHGIRL999:</u> That is so sad for you. But I bet the girls at your school are glad you will be around for another year! :)

<u>JBLACK94710:</u> I don't know what they think.

<u>NORTHGIRL999:</u> Oh it is not mystery, diving board boy. Girls think about nice boys, about boys who care for them and make them feel nice. Like you make Aine feel!

<u>JBLACK94710:</u> I'm glad you feel that way Aine.

<u>NORTHGIRL999:</u> When I am in chat with you Jonah Black it make happy body all over!

<u>JBLACK94710:</u> Okay. How is your boyfriend?

<u>NORTHGIRL999:</u> Good news. I broke up with boyfriend. He go back to Gladanyask, which is small town near Arctic Circle. He do not like big city Stokholm and big city womans.

JBLACK94710: What's not to like?

NORTHGIRL999: He do not like womans with big idea like being in charge. He want me to do what he say. Gladanyask pig!

JBLACK94710: BTW, thanks for sending me your photo. You don't have any of them with your clothes ON, do you?

NORTHGIRL999: Jonah Black not want to see naked Aine?

JBLACK94710: It's not that it's just I want to know what you're really like. It's hard to get a sense of someone when your only picture of them is nude in some sauna.

NORTHGIRL999: Sauna is good place to see naked!

JBLACK94710: I guess.

NORTHGIRL999: If you come to Norway Jonah Black we make love in sauna.

JBLACK94710: That sounds good.

NORTHGIRL999: Uh-oh. Aine has to go now. I send you kiss * * * *. You are my best American!

JBLACK94710: Bye Aine!

As soon as I finished logging off, Honey came in and stood behind me reading the IM. I could feel her smirking. I hate to admit it, but I'm pretty sure Honey's been right all along. Northgirl is definitely a fraud.

"So did you figure out who she is yet?" Honey asked me.

"Not yet," I said.

"She really is shameless. You see there, six lines

from the bottom, she says she's in Norway." Honey pointed. "She can't even remember if she's pretending to come from Norway or Sweden."

"You think I should just tell her I know she's a fake?"

"Depends. Maybe you like getting fake messages from fake people." The way she said this, it didn't sound mean. She said it like, maybe some people like to live in a fantasy world. It's your own choice, I guess.

"You have to admit it's kind of cool," I said.

"But it would be depressing to find out who she really is. She's probably some forty-year-old insurance salesman in Kansas," Honey said.

"I don't think so. I think she's some girl I really know who's just too shy to talk." I was only just deciding this as I said it. I sounded like a perfectly good theory.

Honey smiled. "Well, whatever sad lie you want to believe, Yak Meat. Come on. It's time for dinner."

"You know you don't have to make me dinner. I can fend for myself while Mom is on her book tour," I said. "So what did you make me?"

"Your favorite. Chili dogs and potato chips," she said. Honey uses canned chili, so it's not as labor intensive as it sounds. It's basically heat and serve. Actually, that sounds pretty good.

Oct. 24, 8:15 A.M.

I'm sitting in homeroom and I'm the first person here. Even Miss von Esse isn't here yet, so I'm writing in my journal. The school is unbelievably quiet right now. I mean, it's so quiet the quiet is almost like a sound you can hear.

I'm here early because I woke up early and I just felt like I had to get up and out in the world. I guess I was antsy after being in the hospital so long.

You'd think I could get a ride to school with Honey in her cool Jeep, but I can't because Honey is in the "genius" section, so she gets to come in later than the rest of us morons. So this morning I rode my bike, as usual. And since it was so early, I rode all through Pompano before I got here. I still think this is the most amazing place in the world to live. I mean, I don't know, maybe any place is amazing if you look at it in the early morning with the sun coming up.

I rode through Hillsboro Harbor and then down Federal Highway and cut over to the 14th Street bridge and stopped at the top of it, you know, just looking out over the water on the Intercoastal. There were lots of boats out, fishing boats and yachts and little outboards headed out to sea, and they all had flags flapping in the breeze. Then I headed over to Ocean Boulevard and up north past all the hotels. Then I cut over to the ocean and leaned my bike against a lifeguard tower. I climbed up the tower and looked out at the ocean. Out on the water, Posie was surfing.

I couldn't believe it was her. She looked like this beautiful ocean princess. There aren't many people in the world who can do anything as well as Posie rides a surfboard. I know I can't.

And then, just as I was thinking this, Posie wiped out. The front of her board went up and she windmilled her arms around and the next thing you know there's this huge splash.

I wait for a moment, anticipating the second her head will pop up above the waves and she'll grab her board and paddle out to catch another wave.

But she doesn't surface.

I clutch the railing of the lifeguard tower, desperately scanning the beach and the water. Isn't anybody going to save her?

I'm the only one on the beach. I'm the only one who's seen what's happened.

In a flash, I jump off the tower, and run down the beach. I dive beneath the oncoming waves and swim down, deeper and deeper. I don't see any sign of her. I'm in a strange sort of cavern, and inside it is an old sunken ship. I swim closer and see Posie, lying on the deck with her eyes closed. A fat octopus leg is wound tightly around her neck. I pull out my knife and the octopus and I wrestle furiously. I keep chopping off its tentacles but it won't die. Posie doesn't stir.

"Hey, Chipper," said a voice. It was Pops Berman. Sometimes I think Pops is my personal guardian angel. He climbed up the lifeguard stand and sat down next to me and looked out at the ocean. Posie was back on her surfboard. "How's your noggin?" Pops asked.

"My noggin?" I said. "It's all right."

Pops nodded. He was wearing his red Boston Red Sox hat again, with the big B on it, and a tan windbreaker. He fumbled around in his pockets for a roll of Pep-o-Mint Life Savers and stuck one on his tongue.

"You want a mint, Chipper?" he said. I took one. In spite of the Life Saver, Pops still smelled like peanut butter. He always did.

Pops moved the Life Saver around in his mouth noisily and studied me. "Ya walloped yourself something fierce, didn't ya?" He laughed.

"It's not funny," I said. "I could have broken my neck."

"You're all right," said Pops Berman. "Long as you didn't die, it was funny. You should have seen yourself!" He laughed.

"I'm glad you find it so amusing," I said.

"Well it wouldn't have happened if you'd been concentrating, Chipper," he said. "You started thinking about walkin' the doggy when you should have been thinking about your dive."

"How do you know what I was thinking about?" I said. Pops is completely psychic. It's scary.

He looked at me like I was stupid.

"Okay," I said. "So maybe I was. It's just that I was trying to choose between these two girls. There's Sophie, who's like my dream girl, the one I got kicked out of school for. And then there's . . ." My voice trailed off.

Pops Berman picked up his cane and pointed it at Posie, out on the waves. "And then there's *her*," he said.

— ■ —

"Yeah. Then there's Posie," I said.

"Well, I'm glad you made up your mind. You made the right decision, too." He looked out at Posie with a big contented smile.

"I don't know. There's kind of a problem," I said.

Pops's smile died away. "Problem? I should have known there'd be a problem if it involved you. What is it this time?"

"She's going out with my best friend, Thorne."

"Thorne?" said Pops. He spat a loogie into the sand. "Not that kid with the goatee?"

You know, it's kind of creepy that Pops knows everything about me, and everything about everyone I know. I mean, what is his deal?

"Yeah, that's Thorne," I said.

"Oh, for Pete's sake. What's the matter with that girl? Ain't she got any sense?" Pops coughed into his fist.

"Oh, she's got sense all right. It's my problem, actually. She doesn't know I like her," I said.

"Why not, Chipper?" Pops said, shaking his head.

"'Cause I haven't told her," I said, shrugging my shoulders.

"Right," Pops said. "Well, she can't read your mind, can she?"

"I guess not," I said.

Pops got up and started down the ladder. Halfway

down he stopped. "You know what you gotta do, don't you, Chipper? You better know."

"No," I said. "I don't."

"Oh, you're young and pretty, but you're not too smart. *Tell her*, you lunkhead. What's to lose?" He snarled, shaking his cane.

"You think so?" I said.

"I know so."

Pops reached the bottom of the tower and started walking up the beach. He was humming his favorite old pirate song.

I rode around for a while longer and then finally I headed toward school. I locked my bike up in front of Don Shula and came in here. Now the classroom is beginning to fill up. Cilla Wright and her friend Kirsten are off giggling in the corner. What it is they always find so giggly about everything I don't know. I just noticed that Cilla has these very tiny sweat stains under the arms of her red baby T-shirt, and Kirsten's hair is wet. On the wall there is this big chart of the human body. It's these two transparent people, a man and a woman, and you can see all their veins and organs and bones. The woman looks a little like Miss von Esse, I think. I mean, if she didn't have any skin or muscles. It's amazing if you look at all the junk that is inside us. I mean, people are just full of crap.

———— ■ ————

Today after classes Thorne and Posie and I sat in the bleachers in the natatorium and watched swim practice. I showed up early to say hello to the team, and the guys all got out of the water and gave me big hugs, which was great except they got me all wet. Even Wailer, Posie's ex, who I thought hated me, gave me this giant macho bear hug. Then Posie and Thorne came in, and we sat down on the benches to watch the practice.

I'd kind of hoped that Posie and Thorne wouldn't come in together. I hadn't seen Posie alone since I got out of the hospital, and I was really looking forward to talking to her. But of course Thorne started jabbering on and on about something, and Posie was all into listening, and it was like I didn't even exist!

So I watched my team practice, which was pretty sad. The team sucks. Don Shula High is a magnet school for languages, right? So today I developed a new theory that people who are good at languages aren't good at sports. Of course our team knows how to say the word *sidestroke* in Dutch and Swahili and just about every other spoken language in the world, but unfortunately they can't actually do it very well.

The divers are even worse than the swimmers. There are only four of us altogether. Me (well, if they ever let me dive again), Martino (but he only does one dive), Wailer (he can't dive at all), and Ricky (maybe, if the coach makes him dive instead of swim).

Wailer Conrad is the newest member, and he has no control at all. He can do these little baby dives off the low board, but you can't compete with those.

I still think it's weird that Wailer is even on the team. He joined because he wanted more extracurriculars on his record, which is pretty lame if you ask me. But then Wailer is a pretty lame guy. He used to go up to almost any girl in the school and tell her he wanted to "drop out and live on the beach and make babies" with her. And they all bought it, even Posie, at least for a while. He was such a player. But ever since Posie broke up with him, he hasn't been scamming on any more girls. I guess he's trying to clean up his act or something. Anyway, I still don't see how diving is going to improve his college record, because our team completely sucks.

Martino Suarez is a good guy, but you kind of have to have more than one dive in your repertoire to win a meet.

Meawhile, Coach Davis is trying to get Ricky Anderson to move from breaststroke to diving, but it's not really fair, because Ricky is really good at breaststroke. He's basically being asked to switch from a sport he's good at to a sport he can't do at all, and he's not happy about it.

I looked up into the stands while I was sitting there, looking for that Indian girl I call Watches Boys Dive. She used to watch every practice, but she wasn't there. Did she stop coming because I wasn't diving?

We sat on the bleachers for a little while longer, watching the practice. When Wailer screwed up a back one-and-a-half somersault, which is a pretty easy dive, I turned around to say something to Posie and Thorne. But they were busy sucking each other's faces off. It was so depressing.

I cleared my throat, but they didn't seem to

notice. I was so mad I wanted to push both of them off the bench and roll them into the pool. I cleared my throat again.

This time Posie pulled back and looked at me with a big grin. She didn't look very sorry.

"Sorry to interrupt you guys," I said indignantly.

"Hey, Posie. Look. Jonah's here," said Thorne, like I'd just arrived.

"Oh, Thorne, don't hurt Jonah's feelings," Posie said. She looked a little embarrassed, which made me feel better.

"Hey, you're right, Pose," Thorne said. "I forgot he's all sensitive."

"Shut up," I said. "I just wanted you both to know that Wailer fell off the board while trying to do a back one-and-a-half somersault."

Thorne shrugged. "Is that bad?" he said.

I shook my head. "You guys are going to be completely unbearable from now on, aren't you?"

Posie smiled. I don't think I'd ever seen her look so happy. She was beautiful when she was happy. "Yup," she said. "We're in love."

"In love? Remember this is Thorne we're talking about? The guy who melted the heads off your Barbies with a blowtorch?" I reminded her.

"Hey," said Thorne. "Those Barbies were asking for it."

"You ever think that kissing is like surfing?" Posie mused.

"I know you have," Thorne said, squeezing her thigh.

"Well, it is. It's like a steam-train wave, when the swell first comes up and everything is like, totally electric." She looked like a power switch had been switched on inside her. She was radiating light. "Oh, Jonah," she said. "I wish you surfed."

"Me too," I said.

Posie shrugged and got out her little waterproof diving purse and opened a can of Skoal. "You guys want a chaw?"

"Sure," said Thorne, pinching off a wad.

Thorne and Posie started chewing.

"So Thorne, how's the Zoo? Everything business as usual in the senior class?" I said.

"Yeah, I guess. Except we have a substitute this week. Mr. Bond has been absent for the last four days," he said.

"Yeah? What's wrong with him?" I said.

"Hell, man, I don't know. Maybe he got hold of a bad clam."

"You want to get out of here, Jonah?" Posie said.

"Yeah," I agreed. "It's too depressing. Let's go over to Thorne's house and watch a movie or something." I was kind of sick of hanging around my house.

"My house . . ." Thorne said. He shook his head. "Sorry, man. My house is off limits. Mom's having the kitchen done."

Posie rolled her eyes. "I think Thorne's got some wicked secret at his house. He never lets me go there."

Me neither. I mean, ever since I've been back in Pompano I haven't been to Thorne's new house. I don't even know exactly where it is. He was definitely being squirrelly about it. But there's no point in trying to see the whole picture when Thorne is involved. You just have to hang out and wait until he tells you the truth. Which might be never.

So anyway, we went over to Posie's for a while, and then I left so they could be alone.

(Still Oct. 25, 8:15 P.M.)

Okay, so I'm doing homework and slowly eating this whole can of Pringles. It's like being on heroin or something. I just can't stop. I do one question in calc and then I have to eat five Pringles, then another problem, then another five Pringles. I used my calculator to figure out that if I keep doing it this way I'll be done with the calculus homework right after I eat the last five chips. Who says math isn't useful?

I've been thinking about something, though, and I might as well write it down, although I'm afraid that even writing it makes me kind of pathetic. And I was already feeling pretty pathetic because of the last entry. Anyway, I've been thinking that it's kind of weird that Mom just went off and left us alone for three weeks while she's promoting her book. I mean, I know it should feel like an honor that Honey and I are mature enough to be on our own, but I still think it's weird. I don't even know if Dad knows about it or not. Probably not, since he hasn't called or anything. Not that he would, the loser.

Of course, most people I know would be thrilled not to have any parents around for a few weeks, and I'm not saying I'm not enjoying it. But it's not like Mom is doing this because she wants to give us this big chance to show how grown up we are. She's doing it because her career as an author and a "broadcasting personality" (barf) is skyrocketing. I guess in order for her to have her career she has to kind of ditch us.

Honey has been acting like she's in charge, even though I'm older than she is. She keeps making all these disgusting dinners and using food coloring to make the powdered mashed potatoes blue.

I mean, in a way it's funny. It's like, half the time while Mom is around I wish she'd leave me alone because she drives me so crazy. And now she's away for three weeks and I wish she'd come back.

I told you this was going to be pathetic.

(Still Oct. 25, 9:45 P.M.)

This is weird. I called Mom at her hotel room, in Atlanta, where apparently some local school board is working to have her book banned. This of course has made her sales go through the roof. *Hello Penis! Hello Vagina!* is now number 14 on the best-seller list in Georgia. Amazing.

Anyway, I called up Mom, and guess what? This *guy* answered the phone. When I asked for Mom, all he said was, "Sorry. Dr. Black is resting right now. Can I take a message for her?"

Dr. Black? You'd think that anyone who knows Mom well enough to be in her room while she's resting would know she's not really a doctor. You'd also think anybody who knows her that well would know who I was. I mean, I'm her son.

I just hung up without leaving a message. And now I'm wondering if maybe Mom has a boyfriend. But Jesus, who could it be?

The crazy thing is, the guy's voice sounded familiar. I'm trying to think of all the middle-aged men I know, but I can't think of anyone. There's Mr. Swede, my boss at First Amendment Pizza, but he's Portuguese and has an accent. Plus, he's married. Then I thought of Pops Berman, who's a lot older than forty. It wasn't him, either. I have no idea who it could be.

Also in the news roundup tonight: Honey went out an hour ago with Smacky Platte, the school's biggest stoner/loser. Why she hangs out with him I still don't get. I mean, Honey has an IQ of like, 874. So why would she want to spend her time blowing smoke rings with a guy who wears a leather Aerosmith sun visor?

More later.

(Still Oct. 25, 10 P.M.)

So I just had this amazing experience. Actually, amazing is definitely not the right word. Pathetic is more like it. I should call up Thorne and ask him if I can borrow that clamshell collar back. Except that if I call him up Posie will probably be there, giggling in the background like she does when she's horny.

Anyway, I just called Sophie. I don't even know

why, since I thought I'd decided not to, but I did it anyway. Maybe I wanted to say good-bye.

It's the middle of Masthead's October break, so I knew she'd probably be at home up in Maine. I sat there with the phone in my lap for about a half hour, just trying to get up the courage to call her. I wanted to tell her, *It's all right. I'm not going to worry about you anymore.*

Anyway, it took me forever, just sitting there holding the phone, before finally I thought, *Screw it, just do it.* So I punched in the numbers, and it rang a few times and then someone picked it up and this very rich Yankee voice, definitely her father, goes, "Yes?"

And I said, "May I speak to Sophie, please?"

There was a long pause. Then I heard the phone being put down, and footsteps going down a hallway. I waited on the line for a long time. While I waited I thought I could hear a clock ticking and the pounding of the ocean on the rocks just outside her door. Then I heard these fast smacking sounds, which sounded like a girl's bare feet on a wooden floor, and then she picked up the phone.

"Hello?"

The sound of her voice was like opening the door to a concert hall where a live band is playing. It was like reaching the top of a mountain after a long climb and being blown over by a tremendous blast of wind. It was like having a balloon blown up inside my chest, growing bigger and bigger. I couldn't believe it. After six months of thinking about her, of dreaming about her, of reliving all those brief shared moments with her, there she was in the flesh, completely and absolutely one hundred percent real.

I hung up.

I've been sitting ever since with the phone in my lap. That was probably the last time I'll ever hear Sophie's voice. I guess I'm okay with it, but it's hard, letting things go.

It's funny how you can worry over something for so long, turning it over and over in your mind, and then all of a sudden it's over. It's not anything you can plan. It seems like life is like that in general. Everyone's always planning things, and then nothing ever turns out the way you think it's going to. At least, that's how my life is.

Oct. 26, 3:31 P.M.

Today something pretty nice happened. After school I was doing my delivery route for First Amendment Pizza and I wound up at Cecily LaChoy's house, holding a piping-hot pizza with sausage, green peppers, onions, and extra cheese. When she opened the door, her eyes took on this orange glow, like a werewolf. I don't know, maybe she was just hungry.

Anyway, she invited me in and I said okay, since it was the last delivery of my shift anyway. We sat down in her living room and watched MTV and ate some pizza.

"How's your neck?" Cecily asked me.

"My neck?" I said.

"I mean your head. You know, the accident you had. Are you all right?" she said.

Cecily has the kind of blond hair that was probably practically white when she was five and is now almost brown, with all these different shades of blond in it. Her hips are pretty large, but they look like they're supposed to be that way, like she's just naturally wide. She was eating this slice of pizza, and there was a thick strand of cheese that she couldn't cut with her teeth so she kept pulling the slice away from her and sucking up the cheese strand. But no matter how much she pulled on the pizza, there was always more cheese hanging off it. Finally, she just took a gigantic bite, and then she sat there, chewing away, with these two giant cheeks, like a hamster.

"I'm all better," I said. I wanted to ask her to eat another slice to see if she could do it again, but she didn't look like she was hungry anymore.

"So you didn't bruise your brain or anything?" Cecily said.

"Well, I still get headaches, but I'm fine," I said.

A video for this band called Lemon came on MTV. Five women wearing only their bras and panties were painting an empty room with these giant paint rollers.

"I love this video," said Cecily.

"Me too," I said, although I actually didn't know the band very well.

"You like Lemon?" she said.

"Sure."

"You know they're playing in Ft. Lauderdale next Saturday. You want to go?" Cecily said.

My thoughts were going about a million miles an hour. I didn't know why I was thinking about hanging out with anyone else but Posie. But Posie is going out with Thorne, so why shouldn't I go to the concert with Cecily? I mean, Cecily likes me. She was flirting with me. She visited me in the hospital. She brought me roses. But I don't really even know Cecily. So then I was thinking is it wrong to go to the concert with her when I don't even know if I like her? I was all mixed up.

Cecily kept staring at me, waiting for me to say something. She definitely seemed like an interesting girl. Her hair was in a cool braid, fastened with this clip with all sorts of snakes painted on it.

"Sure, that would be great," I said finally.

"I'm so glad you like them," Cecily said. "Most guys think they're, you know, like, a chick band."

"No, their music is really cool," I said. Then I started listening carefully to the lyrics they were singing. "Girls going crazy, girls having fun. / Girls taking over, together we're one!" *Oh, God. What have I done?*

"The only thing is, I heard the concert was sold out," Cecily said.

"Really? Sold out?" I tried not to sound relieved.

"Maybe you could ask that guy Thorne for tickets? The one who's going out with Posie Hoff? You're really good friends with him, aren't you?"

"Yeah. Actually, I'm good friends with both of them," I said.

"I heard Thorne can get just about anything," Cecily said, like Thorne was the coolest guy in the universe. For obvious reasons, her saying that really bothered me. I wish that Thorne had to struggle once in a while the way the rest of us do.

Anyway, I guess I'm going to the Lemon concert with Cecily LaChoy. I'm not sure how I feel about that.

(Still Oct. 26, 11 P.M.)

I've done my homework, and it's strangely quiet in our house. Mom's in Baltimore tonight. She called around dinnertime to say that her agent told her she might be on the *Today* show.

Meanwhile, here in Florida they're rerunning some of her call-in shows as "The Best of *Pillow Talk*, with Dr. Judith Black." I don't know what makes the programs they're airing "The Best of," because all of Mom's radio shows sound exactly the same. I mean, some guy calls up and asks her something like, is it normal to masturbate forty-five times an hour? And Mom always has the same answer: "Are you being nice to yourself? Because that's what's important!"

I still can't believe my own mother is out there giving all these kids sex advice, when her own son hasn't even had it. It's pretty bizarre. Not that she knows that I'm a virgin. No one knows. Except maybe Honey, and Pops, because they know everything. And I think Thorne suspects. I don't know what Posie thinks; it hasn't come up.

When I talked to Mom I wanted to ask her who answered the phone in her hotel room in Atlanta, but then I chickened out. I guess maybe I don't really want to know.

Earlier tonight, I asked Honey what she was doing for Halloween. Halloween is actually on a Wednesday, so all the parties and stuff will probably be on Friday. Honey said some alumni guy from Harvard is coming to talk to her Friday night. It's like, her interview for Harvard, where she's applying early decision.

"So where are you going to do the interview?" I asked her.

"I'm not doing any *interview*," said Honey. "The loser can just ride around in my car, and do whatever

I'm doing. He says he wants to get a sense of what I'm like, so he's going to get it."

She was smoking a cigarette out by the pool and she threw the butt in the water. I had to fish it out because if Mom found it in the filter, she'd think I was the one who'd been smoking. Mom always blames me for everything. Honey is her little cherub. It's totally ridiculous.

"Honey," I said. "I don't get it. Don't you *want* to go to Harvard?"

"Beats me," Honey said. "They seem all fired up to get me, though. I just want to make sure they know what they're getting. That guy can hang out with me and Smacky. Maybe I'll take him to the Bob's Big Boy and get him a bacon cheeseburger. You think they got Bob's Big Boy up in Massachusetts?"

I can't wait for this guy to meet Honey. It's going to be a pretty interesting Halloween, I can tell.

Today I saw something that made me so mad I only had two choices. I could either punch someone in the face, or just get out of there as fast as I could. Guess which one I picked?

So there I was, sitting on the bleachers in the school natatorium watching the Don Shula High Swim Team flail around in the pool like drowning seals. Actually, the swimmers were doing fine, but the diving is still just a total mess. Now that Ricky Anderson has been recruited to dive, we have a second guy who doesn't know what he's doing on the diving board in addition to Wailer. Plus, we're no longer competitive in breast stroke, since Ricky isn't doing that anymore. Martino Suarez has his one-and-a-half somersault, but that's all he does, over and over, and it drives me insane. It's like he learned it at camp one summer and if he tries anything else he falls into the water on his head. Mr. Davis is trying to teach him not to be a one-trick pony, but every practice Martino just does that same dive, again and again. Watching him is like being stuck in purgatory.

Anyway, I was there showing my moral support for the team, taking notes and talking to Mr. Davis after each dive. He was calling me "student coach," which is a fancy name for making sure all the kickboards and floats are poolside. After practice I went outside, and saw my terrific best friend Thorne Wood sitting on the hood of his car with one arm around Luna Hayes. I wanted to strangle him.

The amazing thing is that he didn't seem upset or surprised or self-conscious about me catching him with Luna. He just acted like everything was cool.

"Hey, Jonah," he said, not removing his arm from around Luna's waist.

"Hi, Jonah," Luna said, looking pretty pleased with herself. At her party last month she confessed to me that she had a huge crush on Thorne. Now she was getting what she'd always wanted. Only a couple of weeks ago Thorne and I saw Luna making out with Wailer Conrad on the beach. I swear,

Thorne and Luna have got to be the biggest sluts in Pompano. If you ask me, they're perfect for each other.

"So, Thorne, have you seen *Posie*?" I said, kind of digging the words into him.

"Posie Hoff?" said Thorne, as if there was more than one Posie. "Nah. Not for a long time." He made it sound like it had been years.

Thorne looked at his watch. "Dang. Hang on a minute, guys," he said. He whipped out his cell phone and punched some buttons. "Hey, Kendra, it's me. Yeah. What's the NASDAQ doing? Okay. Did you buy some of that tech stock like I said? Okay. Cool. Oh, nothing. Just hanging out. I'll talk to you later. *Ciao.*" He put his phone away. "Sorry," he said.

That was when I felt like punching Thorne. But I didn't.

"Are you going to Posie's party Friday?" he asked me. "It should be awesome!" he said.

I hate, hate, hate, hate it that I'm always the last person to find out about everything. I mean, what is the deal with that?? I didn't know Posie was having a party, because Posie hadn't even told me about it. Plus, I'm going to that stupid Lemon concert with Cecily, so I can't go anyway.

I was so upset I was shaking. "I gotta go," I said, and headed toward my bike.

"Wait, Jonah. Hang out with us," Luna called after me.

Us? The whole thing is so bogus.

I guess I already knew that Thorne was a total sleazeball. And I guess that's part of his appeal. It's like, the more sleazily he behaves, the more girls love him. But it's different when it comes to Posie. I'd kind of hoped that Thorne would value his friendship with Posie enough to treat her like the amazing girl she is, instead of just adding her to his collection. But Thorne's not like that.

I can't imagine what it's like for sex to be this incredibly commonplace thing, like it is for Thorne. This is one of those times when I'm actually kind of proud that I haven't slept with anyone yet. But then again, the longer I wait the more important my first time becomes. Sometimes I'm like, screw it, I just want to get it over with and have sex with somebody, anybody, so I won't have to feel all this pressure.

It's like Dad's special bottle of wine. Up in his house in Pennsylvania, there's this wine cellar in the basement, and on the top shelf is this bottle that belonged to someone like King Edward the Seventh or something, which Dad got as a gift from a client one time. Anyway, Dad has this bottle of wine that's like, two hundred years old, which he's saving for some occasion special enough to drink it. But the longer he waits, the more it's like, no occasion is ever special enough. So he never drinks it.

If I had sex with Posie, that would be a special enough occasion.

I can't believe I'm writing this. I never used to think about Posie this way. Now all I do is think about her.

So, do I tell Posie that Thorne is fooling around with Luna Hayes on the side? Or should I just shut up and mind my own business? I honestly don't know. Is everyone's life this screwed up, or just mine?

I got a flat tire on the way into school today. Flat tires suck. I was cruising down the Mile, when suddenly I felt the rim of my front wheel against the road, and I hopped off the bike in front of the Sub Shop and the Mr. Formal store. I didn't have anything to fix it with, so I just started walking the bike to school. I didn't get very far, though, because something told me to stop and go back.

I turned around and there in the window of the Mr. Formal store was this beautiful girl in a gauzy lavender prom dress. It's Posie, or a mannequin that looks exactly like her. And then she says, "Of course I'm not a mannequin, Jonah, don't be an idiot." She steps out of the window and opens a door and inside there is old music playing, like big band tunes from the 1940s.

"Posie, what's going on?" I say.

And she says, "Sshh. Let's get you into something a little classier."

She picks out a light-gray tuxedo for me that is made out of the softest material, like cashmere or something. "The Silver Shadow," she calls it. I put it on, and the two of us look like we both fell out of a black-and-white movie. Posie's dress is strapless and backless and totally shows off her figure, which is amazing. I follow her to the back of the store, and Posie says, "Ready?" and I say yes, even though I don't know what's coming next.

Posie opens the door, and we walk into a huge ballroom. There is a big band in the corner on a raised bandstand and there are hundreds of couples all doing the fox-trot or whatever. I've never taken dancing lessons or anything, but I just take Posie by the arm, and we start swinging all over the dance floor like we've been ballroom dancing our whole lives. We are totally into it, dancing to this weird old-fashioned music, and it feels completely natural, the way she fits into my arms. The whole time we are dancing we are looking into each other's eyes with an expression that says, *I have loved you my entire life. You are my one and only.*

Then Posie leans forward and whispers into my ear, "Jonah, will you take me for a drive?"

I want to explain to her about the whole license situation, but when we get outside there is an old Rolls Royce standing outside the ballroom. Thorne is standing by the car in a footman's uniform, and he holds the door open for the two of us. Posie gets in the front seat and she looks up at me, waiting for me to get in behind the wheel.

"Posie," I say. "You know I can't drive, right? Remember, I had that accident at boarding school and they took my license away?"

But Posie looks at me urgently and says, "Come on, Jonah. We have to go!"

I put my hands in my pockets and pull the insides of the pockets out, and I'm just a guy with nothing in his pockets. Then Thorne takes off his footman's coat and drapes it over my arm and says, "I can drive you, Posie." Underneath the footman's coat he's wearing the Silver Shadow, too, and it looks even better on him. I'm standing there like an idiot, and Thorne puts a shiny copper penny in my white glove, and says, "This is for you, my good man." Then Posie and Thorne drive off in the Rolls together.

When I turned to look back at the ballroom, it was all boarded up and the windows were broken. It looked like it had been closed for years and years. All that was left was me and my bicycle wobbling along on its flat tire.

I had this moment of truth or something with Dr. LaRue at Amerishrinks today. I was sitting in a leather chair, listening to the sound of the dentist's machinery next door through the wall. I thought I heard the sound of that suction hose thing they use to suck the gunk out of your mouth, and I wondered who was getting her gunk sucked and what the dentist looked like. I had a feeling the dentist was a woman, because I kept hearing muffled women's voices murmuring to each other.

"Jonah?" Dr. LaRue said.

"Yeah?" I responded.

"I wanted to ask you some more things about the girl at Masthead Academy. The girl you called last week and had to hang up on," he said.

"Sophie," I said. I thought I'd put her behind me, but Dr. LaRue wasn't going to let her get away without a fight, I guess.

"Yes, I want to know what happened, why you

66

got kicked out. Do you think you'd feel comfortable telling me now?" he asked me.

I thought about this. I wasn't sure if I was comfortable or not. "Well, it's kind of a long story," I said.

"I've got time," he said, and smiled sort of benevolently, like he was the most patient shrink in the world. "But before you begin, I'd like to know how many people know the truth about what happened."

"Nobody," I said. "I haven't told anybody."

"Can I ask you why not?" Dr. LaRue said.

The truth is, I don't know why I haven't told anyone else. It's actually not even the worst story in the world. I mean, I was trying to help someone out and things went wrong. But it's nothing to feel ashamed about.

"Do you want to tell me the story, Jonah?" Dr. LaRue said.

"Yeah," I said. "Okay, I'll try."

Dr. LaRue leaned forward in his chair. He looked excited, like he was thinking, *Yes, we're finally getting somewhere!*

He's a pretty ugly dude. That giant bald head, the tiny little toothbrush-bristle mustache. I try not to look at him too much.

"Well, first I have to tell you about Sophie," I said. Starting the story made me feel like I was

Columbus, or something, leaving Spain. Some hero embarking on an epic journey.

"She was in my class at Masthead. It's this very rich, private boarding school, in the Philadelphia suburbs. I never knew anybody who acted like that before. I mean, the people at that school were from another planet. At least, a different planet from Pompano.

"Sophie comes from Kennebunkport, Maine, the same place as George Bush, you know, Senior. She has this funny Maine accent, it's totally weird. Like she says '*bee*-yah' instead of 'beer.' And '*ev*-ah' instead of 'ever.' I love the way she talks. And Sophie is beautiful. She's got blond hair, and she's skinny, but not too skinny. She always had this kind of aloof attitude, like she was watching everything from far, far away. And her eyes were so sad, like she was keeping all these big, terrible secrets. Like they were green trapdoors to someplace really . . . dark.

"Anyway, I was kind of afraid of Sophie. She was just too perfect. We weren't in any classes together except music, and in that class she sat by herself in the back row. She was kind of a musical genius. One time Mr. Krakow, the music teacher, had us write these percussion pieces for class, and Sophie came up with this whole crazy symphony for woodblocks and triangles. Everybody in the class played it, and it was awesome."

I told Dr. LaRue about that day, how Sophie handed out the sheet music for her piece, which was called *Damnation*, with three woodblocks, and two triangles, cowbells, bongos, maracas, and kettle drums. I was one of the woodblocks. We all played this thing she had written, and it was incredibly intense. Sophie just sat there listening, with this sad expression on her face. I wanted to ask her why she was so sad, but I never did.

"Jonah?" Dr. LaRue said.

All of a sudden I didn't feel like going on. All I could think about was that look on Sophie's face. I wished there had been some way I could have really helped her. I wanted to make her happy.

"Jonah?"

I looked up at Dr. LaRue. He was fingering his little mustache like crazy. I guess he was worried he was about to lose me.

"You were telling me about Sophie."

"Yeah, well," I said. "One time we were messing around in the chemistry lab. And my roommate, Sullivan the Giant, came up with this weird like, potion, that would make any girl who drank it fall in love with the next guy she looked at. Like that stuff in that play by Shakespeare, what's it called?"

Dr. LaRue looked very worried now. "*As You Like It*?" he said, but it was clear from the way he said it that he *didn't* like it. He knew I was lying.

"Yeah, that's it. So Sullivan the Giant goes up to Sophie and gives her this potion in a can of Coke. He says, 'Here you go, Sophie, I got an extra Coke, you want some?' But I grab it out of her hand and yell, 'No, Sophie! Don't drink it! It's poison!' and she looks at me like I'm crazy."

I do remember that look on Sophie's face, when she thought someone was putting her on. Part of it was contempt, and part of it was like she was saying, *Hey, if you're insane maybe you and I have something in common.*

"So I knocked the Coke out of her hand and that saved her from being in love with Sullivan, but then the chemistry teacher, Mrs. Lessing, caught the can and drank it, and the next thing you know, Mrs. Lessing is like, totally in love with me, and she's kissing me and trying to get my shirt off in front of the whole class. And at that second, the headmaster, Mr. Plank, came in, and he saw me making out with Mrs. Lessing, and he just expelled me on the spot. Mrs. Lessing protested, though. Like, she wanted me to stay in school because I was her little chemistry pet."

I looked up at Dr. LaRue, and he was pinching

the top of his nose with his fingers, the way people do when they have an excruciating headache. He looked up at me and said, "Jonah, I don't understand. Do you think it's funny to make up stories in therapy? Is that it? You find this all very amusing? Have you forgotten that your parents are paying for your time here?"

I thought about it. "No," I said. "I'm sorry. I just got to the point in the story where I didn't feel like going on anymore."

"So that's why you make up these stories of yours?" he asked me.

"I don't know," I mumbled. "I guess."

"Do you want to tell me the story, or not, Jonah?" Dr. LaRue said. "The truth, I mean."

"Yes, I want to tell you," I said.

Dr. LaRue looked at the clock. "Well, time's up," he said, shaking his head. I think he was really disappointed in me.

"But wait; I want to tell you," I said. I suddenly realized how good it would feel to get the whole thing off my chest.

"You can tell me next time," Dr. LaRue said.

I walked out into the bright Florida sunshine and got my bike, which has a new tire now. It was a beautiful day. The palm trees were swaying in the breeze, girls with tan shoulders, wearing bikini tops and cutoffs, were walking along the road, and it's October. By now everyone at Masthead is wearing sweaters, and the leaves are crunching beneath the girls' feet as they walk across the campus.

I can see Sophie, wearing a green plaid Masthead skirt and a white blouse, running down a hallway alone.

"Hey, Sophie," I call out to her, and she stops and turns around.

"What?" she says. She looks confused. "Do I know you?"

"No," I say.

She scans my face, looking for clues.

"Am I supposed to?"

"No," I tell her. "It's all right. I don't want to make you late."

"Okay," she says, and she turns and heads back down the hall. She opens the door to a classroom and vanishes from sight.

Posie is standing next to me. She puts her arm around my shoulder.

"You did the right thing, Jonah," she says.

And I realize it's okay that Sophie doesn't even know my name. Everything's going to be all right now.

| Oct. 30, 1:22 P.M. |

I'm in English class trying to pay attention while Mr. Clyde talks about *The Color Purple*, which I've been forced to read five hundred times. I liked it the first two times, but by now I'm a little tired of it. It's like, every time I read it I figure the characters must have gotten a little smarter. Like, this time they won't make the same mistakes all over again. You read a book enough times and you just start getting irritated with everybody, and you want to shout at the characters, *Man, don't you stupid people ever learn anything?*

This morning I kind of had a weird moment with Thorne. I saw him going down the hallway toward the Zoo, and I caught up with him

"So, Thorne. What's the story with Luna?" I said.

73

And he went, "Ladies and gentlemen, the captain has announced we are ready for boarding!"

"What does that mean?" I demanded. "You're going to do her, Thorne? Is that it?"

He just laughed. "It's that clamshell collar of yours," he said. "I guess I owe you, man. Hey, you should write a book, *Jonah Black's Erotic Secrets of Being Pathetic*!"

"But Thorne," I said. "You're going out with Posie, right? What are you talking about?"

"Jonah, man. Are you high? I'm going out with lots of girls!" he said, like that was the most normal thing in the world.

"But Posie is your friend, Thorne. The three of us go back years and years, right? Why would you do this?"

He still wasn't taking this seriously. "They're all my friends," he said. "Life is just one gigantic love fest!" He threw his head back and laughed like this was the funniest thing he'd ever said.

I swing at him with a huge right hook and catch him by surprise. The force of the blow knocks him back against the cement wall, which collapses upon his impact. Thorne falls unconscious, and I examine my knuckles, which are unscathed. And now, out of the hole in the wall, come all these girls who have been held prisoner by Thorne. "Thank you, Jonah!"

they shout as they climb out of the hole. Some of them have been stuck back there for so long, their clothes are tattered and dirty. "You're our hero!" They raise me onto their shoulders and carry me to a room where there is a giant double bed, and Posie is sitting right in the middle of it drinking a glass of white wine.

She looks up at me and smiles. "Jonah, thank God you've set us all free," she says.

I try to be humble because when you are a superhero, that's the way you are. "Aw," I say. "It was nothing."

Then Thorne said, "So what's the deal, Jonah? What are you going to be for Posie's Halloween party?"

I felt my face heat up. "I can't go," I said. "I'm hanging out with Cecily."

Thorne looked like he'd swallowed a nail. "Cecily LaChow?"

I nodded. "Yeah."

"Cecily La Dog Chow? Cecily La Cat Chow? Cecily La Monkey Chow?" Thorne said, clutching his stomach and giggling like an idiot.

"Gee, Thorne, that's a nice thing to say," I said sarcastically.

"Whoa, man. I can't believe what I'm hearing. You're not going to Posie's blowout because you're going to be with Cecily Chow Chow? Why don't you just bring her to Posie's—" Thorne's face froze. "Dude. You're not taking her to that Lemon concert. Tell me you're not going to the Lemon concert; just promise me that."

We'd reached Miss von Esse's classroom, and I shrugged. "I'll see you later, Thorne," I said.

As I went into the eleventh grade homeroom Thorne stood in the hallway watching me like I'd turned into someone he didn't even recognize.

I sat down at my desk, and Cecily turned around and winked at me. For the first time I kind of saw her through Thorne's eyes. It had never occurred to me before that she wasn't pretty, or whatever. I just thought she was sort of different, with her braid and her snake hair clip and everything. But to be honest, I don't care what she looks like. I just really don't want to go to that concert with her. I want to go to Posie's.

The unbelievable thing is that Posie still hasn't invited me. I mean, I've barely even talked to Posie since my accident.

I think I have to stop writing now.

(Still Oct. 30, 4:00 P.M.)

After homeroom this morning, Cecily came up to me and said, "So, is your friend Thorne going to get us tickets for the Lemon show?"

I said I didn't think so.

"Well, I know some girls who are going who have two extra tickets," she said. "Would you mind going to the show with Edie and Linda and Cilla and Kirsten?"

Okay, so those four girls are about the goofiest four girls in the eleventh grade. They never go anywhere without each other, not even to the bathroom. And Edie and Linda have matching pink plastic braces on their teeth. But what could I do?

"That would be fun," I said.

"If you come over to my house at six, we can all go together," Cecily said.

"Great," I said.

The whole time I was thinking, *Is there any way I can get out of this mess?* But any excuse I made would seriously hurt Cecily's feelings, and it would be way too selfish. So it looks like I'm going to the Lemon concert on Friday. I mean, I said I would go, so I'll go. You have to keep your word to people. It's not like the end of the world or anything.

(Still Oct. 30, even later.)

Now it's later, and it's been a strange night. I got back home after doing my pizza route—three pepperoni, one sausage, and two plain—and guess who was lying on a chaise lounge, totally buck naked, by our pool?

Smacky Platte. Ew.

I couldn't find Honey anywhere. Mom is still off on her book tour in Texas or whatever, so I was home alone with a totally naked Smacky. And I have to say, Smacky naked is not exactly a pretty sight. He looked like something somebody had run over with an SUV and left rotting by the side of the road.

I wasn't sure whether to wake him up or if I should just go inside and start making lots of noise so he'd wake up and take care of the situation himself. I mean, what was I supposed to do, go up to him and say, "Hey, Smacky, like, you're naked and everything"?

So I went inside and put some loud music on the stereo, Eminem actually. But no dice. Smacky just kept lying there. Then I started to get nervous, because I was thinking, what if he's dead because he OD'd or something, then it'll be my fault that he didn't live because I should have called 911. But I could see his ribs moving so he was definitely breathing. Finally, Honey pulled up in her Jeep and she went out by the pool, wearing only this black bikini that was kind of baggy on her, like it was too big. And she was so pale, like you'd never guess she's from Florida. She leaned over and gave Smacky a kiss and he reached up with his arms and hugged her. Then Honey sat down on top of him.

I was like, *Hello? Can't you hear the music I'm playing in here? Can't you tell I'm home?*

Then Honey reached around her back to untie her top and just as she was about to do it she saw me looking out the sliding glass door of my room and she shouted, "Jesus, can we get a little privacy around here?"

So I turned off my stereo and went out front and got my bike and rode down to the ocean and climbed up onto my favorite lifeguard stand and sat there watching the ocean for the longest time. And then I had a thought I never thought I'd have.

I wish Mom would come home.

Oct. 31, 5:15 P.M.

Halloween. It doesn't really feel like Halloween, though, because Posie's party isn't until Friday, which is actually November 2. Anyway, Honey and I have this whole bowl full of mini Nestlé's Crunch ready to hand out to the kids tonight. I've eaten like, fourteen already.

Life is starting to get totally weird. Today Cilla and Kirsten came up to me at lunch all giggly, wearing these cropped jeans and these little T-shirts showing their belly buttons. They asked me if it was true I was coming to the Lemon concert with them and I said yeah and then they stood there blushing and giggling. Then Cilla said, "I think it's great about you and Cecily," and I was like, *What about us?* I mean, is there something about me and Cecily that I should know?

And Cilla Wright said, in this kind of intimate voice like we're really close now, "You know, Jonah, I think Cecily incredibly lucky to have you." She looked at me with these big moon eyes and I suddenly thought Cilla is actually kind of pretty, with this short brown bob and these very thin eyebrows. She's a lot prettier than Cecily, anyway.

"Yeah, I guess I am lucky," I said, although I couldn't remember what question I was answering.

Then they went off giggling down the hallway. I saw Thorne duck into the Zoo, and I was left standing there wondering how it was that I wound up with Cecily and Cilla and Kirsten and Thorne wound up with Posie.

I watched the swim team flounder around after school again today. Watches Boys Dive wasn't there, which made me sad. Wailer did this dive I call the Assassination Dive because he bounces once on the board, reaches up toward the ceiling, and then it's like somebody shot him with a rifle, he just falls into the water like a dead weight. It wasn't an accident, either. I saw him do it like, five times in a row. The first couple of times I thought he was trying to do something else and failing. Now I think he was doing it on purpose.

And Martino Suarez did his one-and-a-half somersault.

After swim practice I took my bike and cycled around the Mile for a while, and wound up in Marlin Music, looking at CDs. I went over to where all the Lemon CDs are kept and I looked at all the albums, which basically show these chicks with their clothes falling off, making fists like being naked is some incredibly feminist thing. The owner of the store, this huge fat guy with a motorcycle vest and chains on his belt, looked over at me and shook his head like I was pathetic for liking Lemon. Then this girl comes out of a back room that has swinging doors like in a Wild West saloon. She has thick curly black hair and she comes over to me and says, "Put that crap down and let's take a ride."

We go outside and she starts up her Harley Road King and I get into the seat behind her and we take off down A1A. The bike is seriously loud and the tourists are staring but we don't care. I can feel her ribs beneath my fingers as I hold on to her and smell the leather of her jacket. We ride like that for miles, heading north with the ocean on our right until we get to a bar with bull horns on the door. We go inside, and the place is deserted. The girl turns on the lights above the pool table and says, "Let's play some goddamn pool." I go behind the bar and get us each an ice-cold bottle while she racks up.

"What's your name?" I say, and she says, "Lena,"

and I say, "My name's—" and at that moment I decide my name is going to be Max. And she says, "Good luck, Max." Then she breaks and about half the balls smack into the pockets. There's a cigarette dangling from her mouth and she gets all the way down to the 8 and then she blows the shot. Instead of picking up my stick I push her gently back against the green felt tabletop. She is holding a blue cube of chalk and kisses it softly so that her lips have the faintest blue dust on them. I kiss her on the lips, and everywhere else I kiss I leave a blue trace. Posie's beautiful body is covered in blue lip prints.

"Jonah?" she says.

I looked up and Posie, of all people, was standing in the record store. I was holding a copy of the Lemon CD in my hand and she looked at it and smiled.

"I didn't know you liked Lemon," she says. "Jesus, Jonah, I find something new about you every day."

"I don't really like them," I said. "I hate them, actually."

Posie laughed. "So why are you looking at their CDs then?" she said. "Wait, are you blushing?"

"I'm not," I said, but I could feel my face heat up. It was even worse than the actual blushing, being embarrassed about blushing, I mean.

"I'll tell you why," I said, lowering my voice. "I'm going to the Lemon concert on Friday night. Cecily LaChoy asked me."

"Cecily LaChoy?" Posie said. "No way! You don't have a crush on Cecily LaChoy, do you?"

"I didn't say I had a crush on her."

"Then why are you going with her?"

At that moment, looking at Posie, I couldn't think of a single reason why I'd ever agreed to go. I wanted to say something about the braid in Cecily's hair and her snake hair clip, but I knew it would just sound stupid. And anyway, I *don't* have a crush on Cecily.

I shrugged. "She's nice," I said. "She's been nice to me. She came and saw me in the hospital."

"Yeah, but *I* came by to see you in the hospital, too," Posie said.

"I know, but it's like . . ." I decided I'd try to tell her what I was feeling. It was what Pops Berman had told me to do. "I feel like I never see you anymore," I said.

"What do you mean?" Posie said.

"We never do anything together anymore, Posie. You always used to knock on my bedroom window at night and we'd go out in your boat, or whatever. Now I never see you," I told her.

"What are you talking about? I saw you at swim practice the other day," she said.

"With Thorne," I reminded her.

Posie was just about to say something, but then she stopped. She looked at me sadly and put her hand on my cheek. It felt so good.

"I'm sorry, Jonah," she said softly.

"You don't have to apologize. Things change, that's all," I said.

"No, I mean it. Of course it's hard for you that I'm going out with Thorne. I've been so wrapped up in him I haven't even been thinking about it. I guess I haven't been much of a friend to you, huh?" she said gently.

"That's not what I mean," I said. I still hadn't told her how I felt, that I loved her, and that Thorne didn't care about her the way I did. I couldn't bring myself to say it.

"Oh, Jonah," Posie said. She reached out and hugged me, and I put my hands on her back. It felt amazing. But then she pulled back.

"Why don't you come to my house Friday night, instead of going to that stupid Lemon concert?" she said. "You can bring Cecily."

"What's at your house?" I said, pretending I hadn't heard about the big party.

"What do you mean? I'm having a big ole party. My folks are in Tampa for the weekend. It's a costume party. Please come, Jonah! I'll be so bummed if you don't come." She tilted her head to one side, and her golden hair fell down over her shoulder. I wanted to touch it.

"I told Cecily I would go with her to the Lemon concert," I insisted. "There's a whole bunch of people going. I can't let them down."

I knew I shouldn't have said it the moment it was out of my mouth. But I can never lie to Posie. It's impossible.

"Who?" she said suspiciously.

"I don't think you know them. They're all juniors," I said.

"Oh, my god. You're *not* going with Cilla and the Goobers." She stamped one foot. "Tell me you're not."

I shrugged. My face was burning up. "They're driving," I said. *The Goobers*? Is that really what people call them?

At this moment I thought about how much my life has sucked since I lost my driver's license.

"But this is ridiculous, Jonah. You're going to Lemon with Cecily and the Goobers instead of coming to my party? I mean, do you know how *lame* that is?"

"Well, maybe I can talk Cecily into going to your house afterward," I said. I was kind of pissed off at Posie for being so insulting about it.

"You want to know what Cilla Wright is?" Posie

said. "She's a *flat* wave." She put out one hand, palm down, and drew it through the air in a straight line.

All I wanted was to change the subject.

"How's Thorne?" I said, *speaking of flat waves.* I had this sudden desire to tell her about how I'd seen Thorne with Luna. I really, really, really wanted to. But I couldn't. I mean, the minute I mentioned Thorne's name, Posie's face lit up.

"He's great! He's such a sweetie! You know he bought me these earrings?" She showed me her earrings, which were a pair of little mermaids. They looked cheap, but they were kind of cute.

"Where is he right now? Is he meeting you here or something?" I asked her.

"No, he's over at Luna's," she said. "They're making this big presentation together in Spanish."

"Oh, really?" I said. How can Posie be so smart about everything and not know what Thorne is up to? Maybe she has like, a low boy IQ and a high IQ for everything else.

"Yeah," said Posie. "They're really into it."

I didn't say anything; I just stood there like an idiot.

"What are you thinking, Jonah?" she said.

"Nothing," I said.

"Nothing means something," Posie said.

"No, it's really nothing," I said. "Listen, I gotta go."

"Hey, come on. What's up?" Posie said.

"I said it's nothing. Can't it be nothing up when I say it's nothing? Why does nothing have to be something all the time? Why can't nothing be nothing?" I said, annoyed.

After this incredibly suave speech I headed to the counter with the Lemon CD but when I got there I realized no way was I buying it, so I just left it on the counter and went outside. As I walked through the door I looked over my shoulder, and Posie was staring at me with this strange expression on her face. She looked sad.

The whole way back to Avalon Gardens on my bike I was thinking the ride would probably be a hell of a lot faster if I had a Harley.

Nov. 1, 9 P.M.

Just got off the phone with Mom, who's in Baltimore. She gave some sort of presentation at the Johns Hopkins Medical School, and the place was filled with doctors and teachers and everyone asking her questions about *Hello Penis! Hello Vagina!* I bet they didn't ask her the most important question, which is How come your book says you're "Doctor" Judith Black when you barely graduated from college? But no one asked her. I guess doctors like to trust people, and vice versa.

Anyway, I asked Mom when she was coming home and she said next Tuesday, unless they extend the tour. She's going to be on the *Today* show with Katie Couric next week. I can't believe it.

Actually, I like Katie Couric, even if she is like

forty years old. One time, I saw her doing a Christmas show and she was wearing this little Santa hat and a Santa dress-thing that stopped like, in the middle of her thighs. She was climbing this ladder to put a star on top of the tree, and as she reached up to put the star on, the Santa dress rode up and for just this second you could see that she didn't shave the tops of her legs, and there was this blond hair just above her knees and I was like, *Hmm, maybe I should be a journalist one day.*

I guess I'm finally realizing that maybe my mother has written a book that is making a big impact on people. This whole time I've assumed that *Hello Penis* was just a crappy sex manual for teenagers, but I'm beginning to wonder if maybe there's more to it than that. I guess maybe one day I'll read it. Maybe.

(Still Nov. 1, 11:34 P.M.)

Oh, man. I think I just did the meanest thing I've ever done.

I was lying here rereading the last couple of entries, thinking about Sophie and Posie and then about going to the Lemon concert with Cecily, and suddenly I realized I really couldn't handle going to that lame-o concert with her. I mean, the only reason I was going was because I thought she'd go out with me if I went. But that was when I thought she was pretty and interesting, which I don't anymore. I thought about Cecily sitting by my bedside in the hospital after I got hurt. It was pretty nice of her, but I liked her a lot more when I was pretending to be asleep than when I was awake.

I guess what I really liked was the idea of somebody being in love with me, somebody who actually wants me to want them, instead of the usual stupid one-sided situations I always get myself into.

But it's not fair to Cecily for me to go out with her just because I like the attention. I mean, I'm not in love with her. I don't think I'll ever be in love with her. So then it is wrong for me to go out with her, right?

Anyway, I finally picked up the phone and called Cecily and told her I couldn't go to the concert. When she asked why, I thought about telling her the whole truth, that I'm not attracted to her in that way, that the only thing I really liked about her was the fact that she liked me. But then I realized I couldn't say that to her. So instead I came up with this totally unbelievable excuse about how I had to help out with the swim meet tomorrow. If I was Cecily I wouldn't have believed it; it was such a dumb lie.

I heard her voice crack. "Okay, fine," she said. "Forget it." And then she hung up on me.

I felt like a totally heartless jerk, so I called her back to say how sorry I was, determined to tell her the truth. But she wouldn't talk to me, and this time her father got on the phone.

"Jonah Black, don't call here anymore," he said.

About twenty minutes after that, the phone rang and it was Cilla Wright and she said, "I just want to tell you what a total lowlife loser I think you are," and then she hung up. And right after that, Kirsten calls me up.

"Jonah Black," she said. "You are total dirt, do you hear me? Dirt! Where do you get off breaking Cecily's heart in half, you bastard? You should know that before morning every girl in the junior class is going to know what you did, and no one is ever going to go out with you ever again, okay? Do you understand?"

I tried to interrupt and explain myself, but she just started singing: "'Girls together, girls are strong! Girls with power, all life long!'" And then she hung up.

I sat there with the phone in my hand listening to the dial tone, and then I realized she was singing that stupid Lemon song.

■

So now I'm just lying here around the house feeling depressed. I'm not going to the Lemon concert, and everyone hates me. And I can't go to Posie's party because I said I wasn't going and if I show up now everyone will think I ditched poor Cecily just for some stupid party, and they'll realize what an insensitive bastard loser I am.

Honey is lying outside by the pool talking to the alumni representative from Harvard. His name is Lockwood Winthrop and he's like, thirty-five. Honey asked him if anybody calls him Woody, and he said no, so now she's calling him Woody, which she thinks is hilarious.

She's taking him to Posie's Halloween party. Woody has a Bill Clinton mask. Actually, Honey got them both Clinton masks, but she isn't wearing hers. She got out the same costume she wore last year, which is a black widow spider. She looks pretty good as a spider.

I can't tell what Woody thinks, but he seems to be handling it pretty well.

What I can't figure out is this: Does Honey *really* not want to go to Harvard? Is that why she's toying with this guy's mind? I don't know. Maybe Harvard likes that kind of thing. Maybe the wackier she is the better.

Nov. 3, 12 noon

Here we are on November the third. I know the first of November is All Saints' Day, and the second is All Souls' Day. I don't know what the third is, but it's feeling like All Sex Day. I don't know who the patron saint of sex is, but if there is one I should light a little candle for her.

I went to Posie's party last night after all. In disguise. After Honey and Woody headed out I saw that they'd left the extra Bill Clinton mask by the pool. I picked it up, and then I got this idea. I went inside and I put on my good blue suit, and the mask, and then I looked in the mirror. I was one tall, skinny former president.

Then I got on my bike and rode over to Posie's, but it was too hard to see in the mask so I took it off. About a block from her house I ditched the bike and chained it to a fence. Then I pulled on the mask and headed into the party.

I walked from room to room, and nobody knew who I was or when I'd arrived. I think a lot of people just assumed I was the guy who'd arrived with Honey Black, the Harvard guy.

The party was insane. I was a little surprised, because it was a lot more out of control than I'd expected from Posie. There was a keg in the basement, with a big crowd of people standing around it. Most of the lights in the house were out and the whole place was lit by candles. There was a boom box or a stereo in almost every other room, so you could kind of move from place to place and select your atmosphere. The basement, where the keg was, was strictly hard-core music. Upstairs, in the living room, they were listening to some sort of acid jazz. It was very cool and sophisticated, and Ricky Anderson was sitting at the baby grand piano picking out chords along with the music. Everybody in that room was sitting around the fireplace, with these big smiles on their faces, like they were high as kites. Honey was sitting in there with Woody, and she was doing imitations. First she did Billie Holiday and then she did Bonnie Raitt. I had no idea she had such a good voice. My sister has talents I don't even know about.

The Harvard guy seemed totally drunk. I mean, I don't know what they'd been doing between the time they left the house and then, but Woody couldn't even get a word out without slurring it, and he kept knocking over his wineglass. I wondered if this was all part of Honey's plan. At one point, right after she did this really impressive Aretha Franklin, Honey looked up at me and winked, and I realized that of all the people at the party, the only one who knew I was me in my Bill Clinton mask was Honey.

Later I went into the kitchen, where people were making themselves mixed drinks out of the Hoffs' liquor cabinet. There was this girl Lindsey, who was sort of like the toastmaster or something. She was making these custom cocktails and handing them around. I saw her mix tequila, root beer, and this thick red syrup called Grenadine and give it to this other girl Wendy and she called it a Shrunken Head Float. Wendy sipped it and said, "It's good!"

Lindsey looked at me. "You want one?" she offered. I said no, then she said, "Tell you what, Mr. President, I'll make you something special!" She poured Jack Daniels whiskey and apple cider into a shaker and shook it up and poured it into a short glass and put in one of those red cocktail cherries.

Then she handed it to me. "All for you, Mr. President," she said.

I tasted it and said, "Well, sweetheart, that tastes mighty nice!" Just like Bill Clinton, with an exaggerated Southern accent.

"Taste it," Lindsey said.

So I did. "You mix one mean little cocktail, ma'am. You wanna be my intern?" I said.

Lindsey laughed again like this was really witty. Then she came over to me and leaned against me so her breasts were right up against my shirt, and she said, "Why, Mr. President, I'd love to be your little intern!" Then she turned around and she showed me her underwear, which was a thong.

At that exact moment, Wailer came into the kitchen and he was very drunk. "Yo, Lindsey, you know what I want," he slurred.

"I'll see you later, Mr. President," she said, and then she went and made another Shrunken Head Float for the star of the diving team and I got the hell out of there. I still hadn't seen Posie anywhere.

I left the kitchen and walked sort of aimlessly through the Hoffs' house. I passed by the bedroom of Posie's little sister, Caitlin, and for a second it took my breath away because when I first saw her I thought she was Posie. I always thought of Caitlin Hoff as this little girl in pigtails, but there she was, lying on her stomach on her bed, doing homework of all things. She really did look exactly like a younger version of Posie. I just stood there in my Bill Clinton head, and Caitlin looked up at me in disgust. So I moved on. I guess Caitlin Hoff is a Republican.

It was pretty quiet upstairs. I peed in Posie's parents' bathroom, which felt kind of illicit, even though I'd done it before, but that was when her parents were home. It's a weird bathroom, with mirrors on all four walls and even the ceiling. I looked in the mirror and this infinity of Bill Clintons looked back at me. I wagged my finger at myself. "I did *not* have sexual relations with *that woman*. With Sophie O'Brien. Now if you'll excuse me, I have to get back to the nation's business."

Actually, Bill Clinton is starting to feel like a long time ago. Still, he's hard to beat for laughs. Anyway, I left the bathroom to attend to the nation's business, or whatever, and I heard voices coming from Posie's room. I went down the hall and I thought I heard Posie laugh, so I knocked briefly and opened the door.

And there was Thorne with all his clothes off, on Posie's bed, lying next to Luna Hayes, who was also naked. She was holding Posie's teddy bear, Mr. Tummy.

I stood there staring at them, not sure whether to be embarrassed or angry. Thorne looked back at me with an expression I'd never seen on his face before. He looked ashamed. Like he knew he was doing something wrong but the only reason he'd done it was because he didn't think he'd get caught. And now he was caught.

"B-Bill Clinton!" he stuttered, pulling the sheet over himself.

"Thorne Wood?" I said, pointing at him. I was still speaking in this fake Arkansas accent.

"Yes?" he said.

"Thorne Wood, you are a son of a bitch," I said.

I couldn't think of anything else to say. Luna was holding the sheet over her breasts and looking at Thorne like she was wondering why he didn't just deck me so they could get on with it.

I didn't have anything else to say, but I felt like I had to do something, so I threw the rest of my drink in Thorne's face. And then I left. My body was shaking all over.

I was so mad. Goddammit, what was wrong with Thorne, anyway? He was going out with one of the greatest girls in the whole world, but then he had to go and have sex with some other girl at Posie's own party in Posie's own bedroom? I mean, I'm not a prude or anything, but I do think there are some things that are just plain wrong, and this is definitely one of them. I don't think you can get any lower.

I went back into the bathroom, the one with all the mirrors in it, so I could splash some water on my face. But there was a guy in there washing his hands. It was Woody from Harvard.

For a moment the two of us just stood there, in that room full of mirrors, two Bill Clintons kind of checking each other out. We circled around each other, and everything that he did, I kind of mirrored. Like, Woody put his hand on his nose, and I put my hand on my nose. Then Woody scratched his head, and I scratched my head. It was pretty bizarre. It's funny how people behave differently when they're wearing a mask. I mean, we were being total freaks.

Finally Woody said, "Nice costume."

So I said "Nice costume" back.

Then he said, "You go to school with these kids?"

"Yeah," I said.

"It's different at college," he said. "You'll see."

"What's different about it?" I asked him.

"Well. At college no one knows who you used to be. You can be anyone you want," he said.

"That's good?" I said.

"Definitely. You can kind of make yourself up from scratch. Be the person you always wanted to be. Instead of who everyone thinks you are." He paused. "Women love it. You can be like, Mystery Guy."

"Yeah?" I said.

"Absolutely. The less women know about you, the more they can make up in their heads. They can pretend you're their knight in shining armor. Instead of, you know, just you," Woody said. He tried to take a sip of his drink through the mouth hole in his mask and dribbled some on his shirt. There was a big red stain on his chest from a whole night's worth of dribbling.

I thought what he was saying sounded like something Thorne would come up with. It sounded like a bunch of bullshit.

"So," Woody said. "Have you ever thought about going to Harvard?"

"You know what?" I said, leaving the bathroom. "I wouldn't go there for a million dollars."

I ran downstairs and went outside to cool off. But I couldn't cool off, I was still so mad.

As I was standing there on the Hoffs' stoop Posie came up to me, just out of the blue.

"Is that you, Woody?" she said.

"No, it's not Woody. It's me, Bill Clinton," I said

in my exaggerated Arkansas accent. I was getting pretty good at it.

I couldn't stop staring at her. Posie was dressed as a mermaid, complete with a long fishtail made of interlocking green foil leaves that dragged on the ground. The top half of her body was bare except for a green string bikini top, and her skin and hair were covered in gold glitter. She was all twinkly. She was unbelievable.

"I thought you were inside sitting around the fire with Honey Black and everyone," Posie said.

"No, ma'am." I couldn't get enough of her. I wished that I had come to the party as a fisherman. Or something.

She looked at me and grinned. "You aren't Woody, are you?"

"No, ma'am," I said.

She lifted a little bottle of brandy to her lips and took a good swig. Then she wiped her mouth with the back of her hand. "So tell me, Mystery Man. Have you seen Thorne?" she said.

"I sure as hell have," I said, in my own voice.

"So where is he?" Posie said, not noticing the difference.

"Oh, ah don't know, ma'am. He's inside, or something. I reckon." I reverted to Bill Clinton again, but I couldn't quite remember how I'd done the voice. My anger at Thorne was wrecking my whole act.

"Come on. Where is he?" Posie said urgently. "You know."

"Ah-ah don't, ma'am. I don't . . . ah just . . ." I stuttered.

Actually, at that exact moment I really felt like Bill Clinton, standing there and lying to people. Except that I wasn't the one who'd been having sex; it was Thorne. There I was feeling all the guilt and pangs of conscience for something that Thorne had done.

I looked at Posie, and she looked at me, and for a moment our eyes locked. I couldn't believe she didn't know it was me behind the mask. I mean, couldn't she tell it was me from my eyes?

"Where is he?" she said, quietly. "I need to know."

I suddenly realized that my lying to Posie to protect Thorne made absolutely no sense. I mean, why was I trying to save his ass, given the sorry state of things? But then I realized that it wasn't Thorne I'd been trying to protect all along. I mean, sure, I didn't want Posie to be angry at him, but that was never the point. The point was, I was protecting Posie. I didn't want her to find out, once again, that she'd given her heart to some guy who turned out to be a liar. And I didn't want to be the one to tell her, because I didn't want her connecting the bad news with my face. Wearing a mask made the whole thing a lot simpler.

"Posie," I said. "I saw him in your room."

"In my room?" she said, slowly. "Really?"

I nodded. "He was in there with Luna. The two of them."

"Luna? He was in there with . . ." Posie inhaled sharply and raised her hand to her mouth. "Were they . . . ?"

I nodded again. "Yeah."

"I knew it!" she gasped, stamping one foot. "Goddammit, I knew it. Well, I'm going to go up there and punch him in the goddamn nose. Who does he think he is? I'm going to friggin' keel-haul him, the bastard!"

I touched her arm. "Posie," I said. "Don't be angry. Just forget him. He's not good enough for you."

"You can say that again," she said. She looked down at my hand and then up at my eyes again.

"What you need is someone who loves you," I said. "Someone who realizes what you are."

"Which is what, exactly?" Posie asked me.

"A total miracle," I told her. I couldn't help myself. It was the truth.

She shook her head. "I'm going to go up there,"

she said softly, "and kill him." She spun around and started toward the stairs, then she stopped and turned back to me.

"Hey," she said. "Who *are* you, anyway?"

I hesitated for a moment, and Posie started walking toward me. She couldn't walk very fast because she was dragging her mermaid tail behind her. I turned and started down the flagstone walkway to the street. "Hey," Posie called. She was trying to run after me, but the giant tail only let her take little awkward steps.

I started to run. "Hey! Come back here!" I heard Posie yell, but I was much too fast for her. I couldn't see very well through the mask, so I reached up and slid it off my head. The cool night air felt great, and I threw the Bill Clinton head onto the pavement. The mask made a flumping sound as it slapped onto the sidewalk.

I ran for a block, and just as I turned the corner toward the place where my bike was stowed, I looked back.

Posie was kneeling down on the sidewalk, holding the Bill Clinton mask. I remembered Cinderella's slipper and wondered if Posie would spend the rest of her life looking for the mask's owner, the one man whose face it fit.

Then I got back on my bike and headed home.

I'm getting a ride into school with Honey this morning. I'm all dressed, but I haven't come out of my room. Honey is listening to Mom talking to Katie Couric on the *Today* show in the living room, and she is laughing so hard she keeps falling off the couch.

Katie Couric: What's the most important thing you'd like to say to teenagers, or their parents, who might be listening to us this morning?

Mom: Well, there are a lot of things I'd tell young people. But the most important thing is, there's nothing wrong with pleasuring yourself. It's totally normal. It's a safe way of making yourself happy. Pleasuring yourself!

Katie Couric: You have children, don't you, Dr. Black?

107

Mom: Yes, I do. I have a daughter, Honor Elspeth, and a son, Jonah George.

Katie Couric: And have they read your book?

Mom: Well, I know Jonah has. He's really taken it to heart!

Katie Couric: You mean he—

I clamped my hands over my ears. "I'm not listening, I'm not listening, I'm not listening!" I yelled.

By the time I took my hands off my ears, all I could hear was Honey laughing and rolling off the couch again and hitting the floor.

"Hey, Jonah!" she shouted. "You're going to be famous!"

(Still Nov. 5, 11:45 A.M.)

Study hall. I'm sitting across from this very tiny girl with long brown hair. She is doing homework in a language which I think is Japanese because she's using this inkwell and a quill pen. She keeps drifting off or something and nicking the quill against her lip and making these little black lines on her lip with ink. Now she's coming out of her trance and she's dipping the quill in the inkwell again and making some marks in her notebook but after a moment or two she starts looking out the window again. She's just sitting there with the pen in one hand and the ink is starting to seep into her white shirt and I want to say something.

Okay, she just said, "Oh!" Out of the corner of my eye I can see her looking at the ink mark on her shirt, and she's looking around to see if anybody has noticed. Nobody has except me, and I'm pretending I didn't. Now she's getting up and asking the proctor if she can go to the bathroom, and she's running down the hallway, and I think she's in tears. I can see the pen on the floor where she dropped it and I want to pick it up and draw a message in her notebook, but I don't know how to make the Japanese characters for *Posie You're Amazing*.

I can say it in German, though. *Du bist ausgezeichnet.* But it's not the same.

(Still Nov. 5, later.)

At the end of German class today Miss von Esse said, "There's something I need to talk to you about, Jonah," and the way she said it gave me this big rush. Was she going to give me another chance?

Everyone else had left the room, so it was just her and me. She sat down behind her desk. "Jonah, you know that some of your teachers are upset about what was done to you," she said.

"What was done to me?" I asked her.

"About your being held back. We feel it's a waste of your time to repeat eleventh grade."

"I know," I said. "And you told me if I could get my German grades up you'd ask Mrs. Perella to move me back into the senior class. And then I screwed the test up. So I'm stuck."

She smiled. "Lately it's come to our attention that you've been under . . . some particular pressure . . . at home."

"I have?" I said.

Miss von Esse nodded. "It's not easy to study in a home without any parents."

"I have parents," I said, a little defensively.

"Yes," she said. "But with your father in Pennsylvania, and your mother . . ." She looked confused for a moment. "Where is your mother, anyway?"

"She's on the radio," I said.

"Yes. Well, I understand how hard it must be for you to focus," Miss von Esse said. "Jonah, do you think you could get an A in my class this marking period if you studied extra hard? If you do, I think we can make the case to Mrs. Perella again."

"But she won't listen," I said. "She hates me."

"Jonah," said Miss von Esse, lowering her voice.

"There are a lot of teachers on the faculty here who are rooting for you."

I think Miss von Esse was trying to tell me that she likes me. It was kind of nice, and kind of embarrassing.

"Please, Jonah," she said. "Study for the next test like it's the most important test of your life. We want to help you. But you have to give us something to work with."

"Okay," I promised.

"Okay?" said Miss von Esse. "You'll do it?"

"I'll do it," I said. But even as I said it I wondered if I could. I guess we'll find out.

Oh, there was something else I wanted to write about:

Last night I had kind of a fight with Honey. Or excuse me, should I say Honor Elspeth? It was the wrong time for a fight because I was on my way out the door to do my route at First Amendment, but there she was, lying around the pool with her top off and these weird kind of eye-protector things that look like a pair of hard-boiled eggs cut in half over her eyes. I went out to say good-bye to her and she somehow felt my eyes and she said, "Quit looking at my boobs, Penishead."

"Jesus, Honey, can't you cover yourself up for like, two seconds?" I said.

—— ∎ ——

"I don't want to cover them up. I want to toast 'em like chickens," she said.

She pulled a towel over herself and pulled off the sunshades. "You ever think that sex is like KFC chicken?" she said, squinting up at me.

"No, Honey," I said. "I never thought that."

"Yeah, well, I'm not surprised 'cause it's like this theory that I invented. There's Regular, there's Extra Crispy, and there's the Colonel's Rotisserie Gold."

I shook my head. "Which one's Smacky?" I said.

"Smacky?" she said. "You think I'm doing it with Smacky?"

"Honey," I said. "You *are* doing it with Smacky."

"Oh, but not for real," she said. "That's just, you know, ambient sex."

"Ambient?"

"Yeah, I mean that's like the sex that's just like background noise, like the sex you don't even think about. It's like mashed potatoes or something," she said.

"I thought you said it was like chicken," I said.

"Yeah, well if it's chicken, it's definitely Regular. It sure isn't Extra Crispy," she said.

"Honey, I have to ask you. What's the deal with Smacky? I mean really?" I asked her.

"What do you mean, what's the deal? He's my friend," she said.

"Honey. He's a vedge. He's a total wasteoid. You can speak nine languages. What do you see in him?" I said.

"I don't see anything in him. He's just my friend. Anyway, what do you care?" she asked me.

"You really want to know? Honestly?" I said.

"Not really," Honey said, yawning.

"I'm worried about you, okay? I'm worried you're messing up your life," I said.

She suddenly seemed really angry at me. "My life is plenty messed up already. Smacky doesn't have anything to do with it," she growled.

"How is your life messed up?" I asked her.

She sighed. "You might as well read this." She picked up a letter that was on the ground next to her and handed it to me. It was from Harvard University in Cambridge, Massachusetts.

Dear Ms. Black:

On behalf of the board of admissions of Harvard University, it gives me great pleasure to extend to you this offer of early admission. We had an exceptionally large pool of applicants this fall for the limited number of spaces available. Your accomplishments and academic record clearly distinguished you from—

I looked back at her. "Honey," I said. "You got into Harvard!"

"Yeah," she said. She put the sun protectors back on her eyes and lay back on the chaise lounge.

"Are you going to go?" I asked.

"Yeah," she said. "I guess." She reached down and picked her bikini top up off the ground. She hooked her fingers in the straps and shot it at me like a rubber band. It hit me in the head and fell on the ground again. Then she rolled over onto her stomach.

"You're sad that you got into Harvard?" I said. "I don't get it."

"Oh, I'm not sad," she said, but she sounded sad. "I'll go to Harvard. It's what everyone expects of me. I'll go to goddamn Harvard and graduate first in the goddamn class and I'll become a goddamn lawyer and make a million dollars. Okay? Fine."

"But Honey, that's not a bad life. Is it?"

"No, it's terrific," she said hollowly. "It's exactly what I'm supposed to do. I don't even get any choice about it. It's all written in stone."

I didn't know what to say. "I'm sorry you got into Harvard," I said. "I don't know. Maybe you could apply to some other places and see if maybe *they'd* reject you."

"Yeah, well," said Honey. "I guess it's something to hope for."

As I rode my bike down the front walk Smacky

Platte drove up in his pickup. "Jonah, man. 'S up?" he said.

"Nothing," I said.

(Still Nov. 5, 5:33 P.M.)

Now I'm at First Amendment Pizza, waiting for my delivery shift to end. About a half hour to go. I'm writing at a table in the back. It's very quiet in here. I want to write this as fast as I can, then get back to studying for the big German test tomorrow. I have to ace that test so I can be a senior and finally achieve my rightful place in the universe.

I got here about two hours ago. When I first arrived, Mr. Swede had a whole stack of pizzas ready to go, so I strapped them to the back of the bike and headed out. I delivered the first two pies without anything especially interesting happening, but the third one was to a family named Wright. I wasn't even thinking about this until I rang the bell, and of course Cilla answered the door. She was wearing this purple bathing suit with fringe on it. I'm not kidding, fringe. She's just pouring out of it, and I look at her and she looks at me and she says, "Jonah, I am so glad it is you," and she gets the pizza out of the box and for some reason it's not pizza now, it's like a dozen lemons.

"Hang on, Jonah, let's do this right," she says, and we go into her family's living room, which has cathedral ceilings. Cilla takes off her top and slides down her bottoms and I take off my clothes, too, and the next thing you know we are both juggling the lemons, completely naked. The ceilings are so high that the lemons almost disappear out of sight and we just stand there, the two of us naked, looking up at the sky until finally the lemons rain down on us. Cilla cuts one in half and squeezes the juice all over herself and I go over to help her. She throws her head back and I squeeze a lemon wedge into her mouth and she wrinkles her nose and giggles. "It's tart," she says.

Cilla disappeared for a second and when she came back down the hallway she was wearing a shirt so she wouldn't appear so naked. She took the pizza box from me and shoved ten bucks in my hand. "Keep the change," she said. Which meant that I was getting exactly one penny as a tip.

"Cilla," I said.

"If I'd known you were delivering pizzas for First Amendment I would have called someplace else," she said. She looked like she hated me.

"How was the concert?" I said.

"Just go," she said. "I don't ever want to talk to you. You're mean, Jonah."

"Just wait. Let me explain. Don't I even get to explain?" I said.

"What's to explain? You told Cecily you'd go with her. You told her you liked her. Then the night before the concert you blow her off. What's wrong with you?" Cilla demanded.

Listening to her put it that way, I felt ashamed. Cilla was right. I'd done a really mean thing.

"I never told her I liked her," I said, but I knew how lame it sounded.

"You said you'd go with her. You think she asked you because she hates you?"

"I said I'd go because I wanted to be nice to her. But I really didn't want to go. And I knew she thought it was like, a date. So I told her I couldn't go because I didn't want her to get the wrong idea. You think I should have led her on?" I said. I sounded like my dad, pretending to be rational when I was really being a selfish jerk.

"You already did," Cilla said disgustedly.

"I was trying to keep from hurting her feelings," I said.

"Great job. She's been crying her eyes out for three days!" Cilla exclaimed.

"I'm sorry. I'll call her," I said. I felt terrible. "I don't want her to be sad."

"You leave her alone. You've done enough!" Cilla cried. She shook her head. "You know, when you were in the hospital—"

"What?" I said.

"She went to see you every day. She never said a thing to you about it. But she was so worried." Cilla's lower lip was trembling like she was about to cry. "It was like she was the one who almost died."

I was getting tired of this. I mean, Jesus, give this girl an Oscar for Best Actress.

"I saw her there," I said. "It was very nice of her."

"And this is the way you treat her?" Cilla scoffed.

"But Cilla, just because she's nice to me, just because she likes me, that doesn't mean I can feel the same way. If I went out with her without having any feelings for her, wouldn't that have been worse?" I said.

"Why wouldn't you have any feelings for her? She's nice. She's pretty. She's in love with you. She's my best friend!" Cilla exclaimed.

"I don't know," I said. "It's not something I can explain."

"Something happened to you when you were at boarding school, didn't it?" Cilla said, like she knew all about it. "That's what people say. Something happened and now it's like you're this . . . I don't know what."

"What? I'm this what?" I demanded.

"Nothing," she said, and slammed the door in my face.

I wondered if by nothing she meant that she didn't want to say what she thought I was, or if maybe she thought I was nothing. Like, "Now you're this nothing." I guess it doesn't make any difference.

"Wait, Cilla," I said. I opened the door again, which, looking back on this conversation, proves that I must be insane. "I'm sorry. But was the concert fun, at least? Did Cecily have a good time?"

Cilla glared at me with contempt. "She didn't go. She stayed home."

She slammed the door closed again and I stood there on her stoop, feeling like a total loser. Then I got back on my bike.

I just can't figure it out. No matter what I do I make a complete mess of everything.

On the way back to First Amendment I decided to ride by Thorne's old house. It's strange, I never go by there anymore. But at one point in my life, I used to hang out there all the time.

It was weird to see the Woods' old house with someone else's name on the mailbox. And some family I didn't know was sitting on the front porch, and their kids were playing in the sprinkler out in the yard.

Next door was the motel that his father used to run. It was all boarded up and on the front door was a big sign saying FOR SALE BY PUBLIC AUCTION.

It looked like nobody had been there for years and years.

Nov. 6, 4:30 P.M.

The day after an unbelievable night. I think my life has been changed forever. Okay, here's what happened.

Last night I was lying in bed, studying for the German test, trying to do just what Miss von Esse said, to study like it's the most important test of my life. Suddenly I heard a motorboat out on Cocoabutter Creek, the engine cut, someone walking quickly across the lawn up to my sliding glass door, a knock.

"Jonah. It's me," she said. "We gotta cruise."

"Posie," I said, completely surprised. It was just like old times, Posie showing up in her boat unannounced. I was so happy to see her.

"Come on," she said, and turned to head back to her boat.

I paused for half a second, looking guiltily at my German textbook. I still had a ton of reviewing if I wanted to ace the test, but I've never been able to say no to Posie.

I grabbed my sweatshirt and went outside. Posie had already started up the boat's engine. I jumped over the gunwale and hauled the rope off the cleat and off we went.

"What's up?" I said.

"I'll tell you in a minute," she said. "Right now I just want to cruise."

Posie steered the boat over to the Intercoastal and then up to Lighthouse Point and under the drawbridge, and soon we were headed out to sea. Posie's face was lit with blue light from the instrument panel, and her hair streamed out behind her. The sky was clear, and a huge moon was shining down on the sea.

We went out maybe half a mile from shore and then Posie said something I didn't hear, and I said, "What?" She cut the engine and we just drifted for a moment on a wave of momentum. Then the boat settled down, rocking gently, on the huge quiet ocean. Posie's hair was fluttering softly in the breeze, which was still warm even for November. There were traces of gold glitter left over from Halloween in her hair and on her neck, and they sparkled in the moonlight.

Posie looked at me. "I'm in trouble, Jonah," she said.

"Tell me about it," I said.

"First of all tell me how the Lemon concert was," Posie said.

I really didn't want her to know about Cecily or anything I'd done. And I felt kind of embarrassed for tattling on Thorne at her party, even though I knew in my heart it was the right thing to do. I just didn't want her to know it was me who had done it.

"It was fine," I said.

"How're things with Cecily? I guess this means you're going out now, huh?" Posie asked me.

"I'm not going out with her," I said.

"Why not?" she said.

"I don't know. She's nice but . . . she's just not for me," I said.

Posie smiled, and her smile was like the sun breaking through the clouds. "That's what I thought all along," she said. "I'm glad you're not dating her. Now I don't have to pretend to like her."

"Well, I feel pretty bad for letting her down," I said. "Even though I don't want to go out with her, I still feel like an idiot for hurting her feelings."

"You're doing the right thing, Jonah. You can't go out with someone just because they want you to," Posie reassured me.

"Yeah, well, it's nice to be wanted by some-body," I said, feeling a little sorry for myself.

"Oh, Jonah, there are plenty of girls who want you. You're just not looking." Her face looked like it was going to shatter, like thin glass.

I looked at her. "What's wrong, Posie?"

"I had this weird time at my party," she said. "I mean, it was fun and everything. Everybody was there." She paused. "Everybody except you, I mean."

She reached into a cabinet underneath the steering console and pulled out a tin of chaw and stuck a wad of it in her cheek. "But then at like eleven o'clock, I couldn't find Thorne anywhere. I went downstairs and outside, but he wasn't around. Finally, I was out near the front deck, and I ran into this guy."

"Who?" I asked, acting all oblivious.

"Well, that's the thing, he was in disguise. He had this big Bill Clinton head on, and a coat and tie? At first I thought it was Woody, you know, your sister's Harvard interviewer, because I'd seen him before with the same mask. But this wasn't him. It was some other guy, and you know what he said to me?" she asked me.

"What?" I said, still playing dumb.

"He said that if I wanted to find Thorne I could find him up in my room. With Luna Hayes."

"You're kidding," I said, trying to sound like this was news to me.

"That's what he said. But that wasn't the weird part," Posie said.

"What was the weird part?" I asked her, my heart pounding.

"He said that I should ditch Thorne. That what I need is somebody who knows what I am. And you know what he said I was, Jonah?" Posie said.

"Uh-uh," I said, although I knew. I definitely knew.

"A miracle," she said. Her voice cracked while she said it, and she looked away from me.

"Wow," I said. I felt like such an idiot. Why was it only possible to express what I felt for Posie when I was wearing a Bill Clinton mask? "So who was this guy?"

She looked at me and took my hand. The little boat was rising and falling on the waves. I think my heart stopped beating.

"Well, at first I thought it was Woody the Harvard guy. Then I thought maybe it was Wailer, but he wasn't huge enough for Wailer. I mean, it was just this total mystery. And then I realized there is only one person in the world who could think that I'm a miracle. And the way I know is because I think he's a total miracle, too," she said quietly.

She took my other hand and drew her face very close to mine. Her breath flashed on my throat.

"Um, Posie," I said. "Uh, I'm trying to figure out who you're talking about."

She was so close to me now our lips were practically touching. I put my arms around her back. She looked into my eyes like she was trying to read my mind.

"Jonah Black," she said, almost whispering. "You didn't go to any stupid Lemon concert on Friday night, did you?"

Honestly, at that moment Posie was absolutely the most beautiful thing I had ever seen. All those years growing up she was my friend, the little girl who used to play with fireworks and gunpowder. For the first time I saw her as a woman, strong and fierce and soft and delicate and looking at me like I was the most important person in the world. Actually, it made me feel a little seasick.

"It's true, isn't it?" she said. "Tell me it is."

I answered her with my Bill Clinton voice. "It just depends on what your definition of 'is' is," I said.

Then Posie kissed me. Kissing her was like losing gravity and suddenly becoming weightless, floating above everyone's heads. The boat rocked up and down on the waves, and we kept kissing and kissing like we never wanted to stop. I couldn't get enough of her.

"I meant what I said," I told her, when we finally stopped for breath.

―――――― ∎ ――――――

"When?"

"You are a miracle," I said.

"I think you are," she said. "I think *we* are."

Posie reached down and grabbed the bottom of my sweatshirt and pulled it off over my head. My T-shirt came with it. She put her palms on my chest and rubbed it, like she was smoothing in lotion. My whole body was standing on end.

Then I pulled her windbreaker and T-shirt off, and there she was in her white bra. She reached behind her and unhooked her bra and the next thing I knew her bra was lying over the steering wheel of the boat and there she was. She definitely isn't a little girl anymore.

We pulled off our shorts, laughing and staggering around like we were drunk out of our minds because we couldn't stop looking at each other. And then I grabbed her and pulled her down on top of me. The bottom of the boat wasn't exactly comfortable, but we didn't care. We lay against one side and put our feet up on the gunwale of the other side and kissed until our lips got tired. Then we stopped and looked up at the sky, just holding onto each other. Big gray clouds began to cover over the stars, but I didn't even notice. I was in a daze of happiness.

Then we started kissing again and each kiss was

——— ■ ———

like this amazing conversation with somebody that understands you better than you understand yourself. Posie kissed my neck and my ears and my chest and the hair on the back of my neck stood up like cornstalks and I shivered all over. She put one finger in her mouth and made little wet trails on my forearm with it. I was going crazy.

Then she said, "It's your first time, isn't it, Jonah?"

I couldn't answer her. I was embarrassed.

"It's okay," Posie said. "I'm glad it's with me."

"Me too," I said.

"So what do you think? Are you ready to do it? Let's do it, okay?" she said. "Please?"

I know this sounds stupid, but right then I felt as if I had left my body and I was hovering above everything like an angel, watching me and Posie getting ready to have sex. I mean, it was like my whole life had been building up to that moment. I thought about the times I'd watched Posie surfing and the funny look she gets in her eyes just before she spits out some tobacco juice. I thought about the first time I'd seen her when I came back from Pennsylvania, and how I didn't even recognize her because she'd become so beautiful. And then, for no reason that makes any sense I thought about Sophie. Sophie crying outside the Great Hall at Masthead Academy.

"Jonah, what's wrong?" Posie said, searching my face worriedly.

I shook my head. "Nothing's wrong. I'm happy," I said.

"Your face just went funny. You were thinking about something," she said.

"It was nothing," I told her, running my hand through her hair.

"Tell me," she said quietly. "Tell me."

I looked out over the side of the boat, past the gunwale where our four bare feet were sticking up into the air. I noticed that the sky was darker than it had been before. I also noticed that I couldn't see any land.

"I don't know," I said dreamily. "I was just wondering where we are, I guess."

"We're about a half a mile off of Pompano," Posie said. She pointed. "See the Lighthouse over . . ." She let her hand drop. "That's funny."

"What's funny?" I said.

Posie got up and crouched over the bow of the boat. "Jonah, didn't you drop the anchor?" she said, sounding nervous.

"Me? When would I have dropped the anchor?" I said, sitting up.

"I asked you to. Remember? Just before I stopped the engine," Posie said.

"You didn't. I mean, I didn't hear you," I said.

"Jesus," Posie exclaimed, looking around wildly.

I stood up and looked around. There wasn't any sign of land. Big waves were picking us up and down. The waves were like going up a hill in a little car.

"Dammit, dammit, dammit," Posie said, on the verge of tears. "We've been drifting all night. I can't believe this."

She pulled on her panties and her shorts and her shirt, and picked up the radio in the steering console.

"Wait, Posie," I said. "What are you doing?" I don't know what I was thinking. I guess I didn't mind being lost at sea. All I wanted was to kiss her again. And I wanted to have sex.

"KYX Florida three niner seven this is *Little Wing*, do you read me over?" Posie said into the handset.

There was a crackling from the radio. I felt some spray on my back and realized it was rain.

"Christ," wailed Posie.

I put my clothes on. It was the saddest thing I'd ever done in my life. I'm serious.

"KYX Florida three niner seven this is *Little Wing*, do you read me, over?" Posie repeated.

"Posie?" said a gravelly voice on the other end. Her father. "Thank God. Where in hell are you? Are you all right?"

"I'm okay, Dad," Posie said. "I'm out in the boat with Jonah. We kind of fell asleep out here."

"Where are you? Are you in the Ditch?"

"No, Dad. We're . . . we're in the ocean. We turned off the engine. We didn't put the anchor down. We're not really sure where we are," Posie told him.

"Jesus, Posie!" her father said. "Don't you have any goddamn sense at all? What's wrong with you?"

"Don't yell at me," Posie said, her eyes filling with tears. "Dad, we're lost. We're in trouble."

"All right, all right," said her dad. "Calm down. I'll call the Coast Guard. Where were you when you turned off the engine?"

"A mile off Lighthouse Point," she said.

"What time was this?" he said.

"About one A.M."

"Jesus!" Mr. Hoff growled.

There was a long pause. Posie started to cry. I put my arm around her.

"Okay, Posie, keep this channel open. I'm going to call the Coast Guard. I'll be right back, okay?" he said.

"Okay."

Posie put down the handset. "How could we be so stupid!" she cried, and whacked her hand against the steering wheel. Her bra was still hanging off it, and it fell onto the floor. I reached down to pick it up.

"Give me that," she said angrily, swiping it out of my hand. She pulled her arms out of her shirt, strapped herself back into the bra, and put her shirt back on.

"We're dead," Posie said. "Dead!"

"It's all right," I said. "At least we're together." I really didn't mind what was happening. I wasn't scared at all. It was like I was stoned or something.

"Look at those waves," Posie said, pointing at the water. "Monster barrels." I wasn't quite sure what she meant, but if Posie was scared, I knew I should be, too. I mean, Posie knows things about waves that nobody else knows.

The rain started coming down hard. The waves were almost four feet high. They slapped against the bow. We were getting drenched.

"Posie," said her dad, on the radio. "Are you there?"

"I'm here," Posie said. Her voice was very small.

"I want Jonah to set off a flare. Ask him if he knows how."

She looked at me. "He wants to know if you know how to set off a flare."

"Tell him yes," I said. Somehow I took this incredibly personally. Why would people think I was the kind of person who wouldn't know how to set off a flare?

"Where are they?" Posie asked her father.

"Under the captain's chair. In a red box," Mr. Hoff instructed.

"I've got them," I said. I got out a flare and lit it with the lighter that was in the box and held it over my head. A second later it shot out of the cylinder in my hand and soared above us, exploding like beautiful red fireworks. I smiled and put my arm around Posie.

She shrugged off my arm. "Goddammit, Jonah, not now," she snapped.

It's like there's this curse on me. For the first time in my life a girl looked in my eyes and said, "Let's do it," and not only that, it was Posie. And then, of course, there was this big disaster at sea. I mean, would it have been so wrong for us to have sex first, and then radio in for help? I mean, if you're lost, you're lost. You might as well have sex first.

The radio crackled. "Did you set it off?" her dad asked.

"Yes," said Posie.

"Okay, wait a minute. Hang on." There was a long silence. Then her dad came back.

"Okay, they've got you," Mr. Hoff said. "There's a fishing boat less than a mile away from you. They're coming to get you."

Posie sighed, and I felt a whole layer of tension

fall from her. She started to shake. "We're going to be okay," she said, and only then did I realize that Posie had actually considered the possibility that we *wouldn't* be okay. I put my arm around her again. I felt bad. Missing out on sex didn't seem like the end of the world anymore. I just wanted Posie to feel better.

Soon we could hear the whine of the fishing boat's motor, and then a bright beam of light shone through the night onto our little boat.

"Dad," Posie said into the radio. "We see the boat. They see us. We're all right. I'll see you in an hour or so."

"All right," he said. "I'm glad you're okay. We'll talk when you get home."

Posie turned to me and said softly, "We're rescued."

The fishing boat looked like something out of a Cuban boatlift or something. I mean, it was really old and patched up and barely seaworthy. The fishermen were probably trawling for pretty much any trash fish they could find and selling them as cat food. Two men in yellow slickers were on deck. One of them was holding a knife and gutting a bluefish that was swinging from a winch. There were guts all over the deck and blood on his slicker.

"Thorne?" Posie said.

The man with the knife looked at Posie, and then at me, and then at the other man, Thorne's dad. They pulled alongside of us and tied up the *Little Wing*.

"Posie!" said Mr. Wood. "How are you, honey? Jonah Black? Good to see you, son."

"Thorne?" I said.

Thorne just looked at us like someone had cut off his tongue.

"I thought you were working on your dad's boat," I said.

"He is," said Mr. Wood. "Welcome aboard *The Scrod*, mateys."

"*The Scrod*," I said, looking at the boat. There were piles of fish guts everywhere. "It's . . . I mean, it's . . ."

Posie hugged Mr. Wood. She got guts all over her windbreaker. "It's the most beautiful boat I've ever seen."

She went over to Thorne. "Thank you," she said to him, and kissed him, too. He was still holding the knife. "Thank you for rescuing me."

"Thorne, let's hose this bucket down and get these two some coffee," Mr. Wood said. "Understand you've both had quite a scare."

Thorne glanced at me and then at Posie, and in a second it was like he knew everything. He held out the knife and pointed it at me.

"You're Bill Clinton," he said.

Thorne's dad frowned at him worriedly. "Come on, son," he said. "Let's hose down the deck."

Thorne didn't move.

"Thorne!" Mr. Wood commanded. "Now, that's an order."

"Yes, sir," Thorne mumbled. He unwound the hose and started cleaning the entrails off the deck. Meanwhile, Mr. Wood led us down into the cabin, where he wrapped us up in blankets and poured us some coffee out of a big thermos. I don't usually drink coffee, but this morning it tasted like the best thing in the world.

Mr. Wood got on the radio and told the Coast Guard that we were all right, and then he got back behind the wheel and headed toward Lighthouse Point. We were something like four miles out at sea. Thorne didn't come below deck.

"He told me he worked on a sailboat," I told Posie. "He told me they were giving rides to tourists."

"He told me it was a catamaran," Posie said. She took my hand. "Poor baby. He had to find out about us and now we've found out about him."

"Poor baby?" I said, horrified. "This is the guy who was cheating on you with Luna, remember? I mean, like from practically the first day you started seeing each other. And you're calling him poor baby?"

"What can I say?" Posie said, shrugging her shoulders. "I feel sorry for him."

"You know, Posie, you're really something," I told her.

"You have to have sympathy for people, Jonah," she said. "Things are hard enough anyway." She looked at me. "You aren't feeling bad, are you?"

"About what?"

"About us. About tonight."

"Well, no, it's just . . . I wish we'd, you know. Done it," I said, blushing. I felt really stupid.

"Done it?"

"Made love." As I said it, I realized there was no reason to feel stupid. I was with Posie, my friend.

"Oh, that." Posie laughed and waved her hand like it was nothing. "There's plenty of time for *that*!"

I don't know why, but this struck me as the best thing I'd ever heard in my life. Maybe I was worried that Posie would only be interested in me way out in the middle of the ocean, away from everything. But when she said that, it sounded like she imagined just what I was imagining: a whole future, with the two of us together, having sex whenever we wanted.

"I love you, Posie," I said.

She smiled. "Well *duh*."

Then we kissed again. We kissed for a long time.

When we finally stopped, I looked up. Thorne was standing at the top of the ladder, looking down at us, and it looked like he was the one who was lost at sea.

There is one other not so great result of last night. I didn't get to finish studying for the German test, and I totally screwed it up today. Which means, once again, I'm stuck in eleventh grade, and this time it's for good. But the thing is, now that I'm with Posie, I honestly don't care.

■

I'm in Miss Tenuda's class and we are stranded in the most boring part of American history, the dead zone between the Founding Fathers and the exciting rush up to the Civil War. It is so totally depressing that I'm doing this whole year of school over again, but I don't care. Now that I have Posie, nothing else matters. I'd repeat eleventh grade a third time to be with her.

I have to say Miss Tenuda has been acting a little strange. She keeps pausing in the middle of a sentence and to look out the window, and we're not sure if she's ever going to start talking again. Not that that would be so bad.

I have to write about what happened after I got home from my night at sea with Posie. I got back to the house around eight in the morning. And when I walked into the kitchen, Mom was there, back from her book tour. She was just arriving, so she hadn't been up all night worrying about where I was or anything.

I went over and gave her a big hug. It was weird how glad I was to have her back.

Mom hugged me hard and then stepped back to give me a once-over. "Jonah, look at you! I can't believe how you've grown," she said. She got up to put the kettle on the stove and then turned around, beaming proudly at me.

I kind of liked that Mom said that. I felt like I *had* grown since I'd seen her last. So much had happened.

"How was the book tour?" I said.

"Fantastic. Amazing," she gushed.

"Great," I said. "I'm glad."

"Listen, Jonah," Mom said. "There's something I want to tell you."

"What?" I said.

She seemed nervous, and I wondered if what she had to tell me had something to do with the guy that had answered the phone in her hotel room.

"I just wanted you to know that you're never going to lose me," Mom said. "I'm always going to love you, and I'm always going to be your mom."

"Lose you?" I said. "Why would I lose you?"

"Because I might become famous. I mean, you've never had to share me before," she said, her eyes shining. She looked really happy.

"It's fine, Mom. I'm glad you're famous," I said.

"Really?" Mom said. It seemed as if I'd touched her deep inside. Her eyes were tearing up. "Really really?"

"Yes, Mom, really," I said. "It's exciting."

"Oh, I'm so glad you feel that way." She sighed. "I was afraid you'd experience it as loss. You know, recapitulate in your unconscious the dynamics of your father's and my divorce?"

I had absolutely no idea what she was talking about. Mom always uses that self-help mumbo jumbo. It's the only way she knows how to communicate. I hugged her again. "I love you, Mom," I said.

Tears began to spill down her cheeks. "That is such a validating thing to hear," she said.

"I know it," I said.

She dabbed her eyes with a table napkin. "You'll be glad of my other news, then," she said.

"Other news?" I said. Again, I thought of the guy on the phone.

"My publisher called. They want me to write a sequel to *Hello Penis! Hello Vagina!*"

"Really? A sequel?" I said, trying to sound excited.

"Yes! It's going to be called *Hello, Pleasure: Dr. Judith Black's Guide to Being Nice to Yourself*," she told me excitedly.

I tried to think of a good response. I was glad for her. But writing another book means she'll be working even more than she already is. I know it sounds like I'm this big baby, but I kind of wish she would realize that Honey and I need her to look out for us, too.

"That's great, Mom. I'm proud of you," I said, knowing it was what she needed to hear.

"Are you really?" she said. "Really?"

I nodded. "Really," I said.

As I got up and went to my room, I kind of wished I felt as comfortable talking to my mother about my own relationships and stuff as everyone else in the world seemed to be. Maybe I should call in to her radio show and disguise my voice. Or maybe not.

I stopped in Honey's doorway. She was wearing a black halter dress and reading some book of poems by Allen Ginsberg, in French.

"Hey," I said. "Did you tell Mom you got into Harvard?"

"Oh, no, I forgot." Honey raised her voice. "Hey, Ma, I got into Harvard!" She got up and went down the hallway to Mom's room and opened the door to her bathroom. "Hey, Ma, I got into Harvard."

I heard my mother say something, and then Honey closed the door.

She turned to me. "She's takin' a dump," Honey said. "She says she's glad for me, though."

Nov. 8, 5:15 P.M.

Okay, so it's just me and a can of Pringles again. This time they're barbecue flavored. And Honey got this amazing salsa called Captain Bob's Cactus Explosion, which makes tears come out of your eyes just by smelling it. So I'm eating one potato chip dipped thoroughly in Captain Bob's and then I sit and wait for the top of my head to explode. It takes a while for the pain to subside, and then I do it all over again.

I've been thinking about Thorne these last couple of days. I haven't seen him, and when I tried calling him, I got an operator saying the number had been disconnected. Does that mean the Wood Rendezvous Service, or whatever it's called, has gone out of business? I'm still pretty mad at

Thorne, but I'm worried about him, too. I mean, even after everything he's done, he's still my best friend.

What amazes me about Thorne is that he's actually really poor. All this time he's been pretending he's some millionaire playboy, while he hustles for money all the time. And nobody—none of the girls he's seeing, not even Posie or me—knew anything about it. The idea of him working every weekend on the *Scrod*, cleaning fish—it kind of breaks my heart.

And what about all that bullshit about trading stocks and talking to Kendra on the phone? I bet that was all made up. He doesn't have any stocks. There wasn't even anybody on the other end of the line. It was all completely bogus. I feel so bad. I mean, why couldn't Thorne tell me the truth?

Of course, now that I've written that, I realize I haven't told him the truth about what happened to me at Masthead. I guess we're even. And I guess I understand Thorne. It's a terrible feeling, to be ashamed of who you are.

I have now finished this whole can of potato chips. I wonder if we have any more?

Nov. 9, 4:15 P.M.

This is just a short little thing but I feel like writing about it anyway. Something happened on the way home from school today that made me feel like superman or something. I was riding my bike south on A1A and suddenly I was like, I think I'll stop in at the drugstore. So I pulled over and locked the bike and went into the CVS.

I hadn't even thought about what I needed but the next thing you know I'm in the "intimate needs" section and there in front of me is this whole wall of condoms and stuff. So I started checking out the condoms. I felt really nervous. I mean, there's nothing wrong with buying condoms, but my heart was pounding in my throat and I was afraid some FBI agents were going to spring up out of nowhere and say, *Okay, son, what have you got there? Condoms? Does this mean you're having sex? Are you aware of the implications of that, son?*

Yes, officer. I'm aware of the implications.

And then I thought about what condoms actually are—just slimy pieces of rubber, and I was like, yuck. I don't want to touch Posie with one of these. But still, they're one of the necessities of the life I appear to be living now. And guess what? I like this life!

Anyway, buying condoms is really just the same as buying soap or toilet paper or something. It's like, you pull into a CVS and get your condoms and your candy and your gum and your shampoo and you go out into the world and it's all just routine. But to actually need condoms because I was going to have sex with Posie was more than just routine; it was the best feeling in the world.

I grabbed a pack and started heading toward the counter, but then I stopped and went back because I wasn't sure I was happy with the ones I'd picked out. I mean, there were so many choices. Ribbed. Lubricated. Extra Long. Super Natural. Lite Touch.

I thought I might as well be prepared, so I bought one of each. Then I brought them up to the front of the store and put them on the counter and the kid working the cash register just looked at the condoms and then at me, and he said, "Will that be all?"

"Yes, that's all," I said. He beeped them through the scanner and on the cash register monitor the words lit up: TROJAN CONDOM 2 PCKG, and I felt this huge rush of happiness. I kind of wished there were people behind me in line to witness it. The thing that made me feel happiest of all was how incredibly right it was. I mean, I was just a guy buying condoms so I can sleep safely with the girl I love, and there was nothing extraordinary about it at all to anyone but me because the girl is Posie and the guy is me. Jonah Black, Teenage Stud. Ha!

And another thing. I didn't think about Sophie once today. All I do is think about Posie. She and I are real!

AMERICA ONLINE INSTANT MESSAGE
FROM NORTHGIRL999, 11-9, 9:47 P.M.:

NORTHGIRL999: Hello Jonah Black!

JBLACK94710: Hi Aine! Where have you been?

NORTHGIRL999: Your Aine has been traveling all around. I left Sweden and went to England for my vacation. It is very nice there.

JBLACK94710: What did you see in England?

NORTHGIRL999: I was in London. I saw Westminster Abbey and Buckingham Palace.

JBLACK94710: Did you like it there?

NORTHGIRL999: I liked it but English men are so rude men! Always with the bosoms they go!

JBLACK94710: How do you mean?

NORTHGIRL999: Oh it is as if they have never seen blond girl with bosom before. I go into pub and all the men buy me lots of drink and soon I am a drunken Aine! Very funny situation!

JBLACK94710: You know, Aine, I have to say, sometimes I find it hard to believe some of the things you say.

NORTHGIRL999: What is hard to believe?

JBLACK94710: I don't know. I mean I'm not trying to be rude but sometimes I feel like you're making a fool out of me.

NORTHGIRL999: How can Aine make fool out of Jonah? Aine loves Jonah!

JBLACK94710: I know. I love you too Aine. It's just all a little far-fetched, you know?

NORTHGIRL999: Fetched? What is this fetched?

JBLACK94710: Never mind. I should go.

NORTHGIRL999: No, Jonah. Do not go. I wish not to have my Jonah think Aine is this fetched.

JBLACK94710: It's just that some of the things you say don't make sense. Like you say you're at the University of Stockholm in Norway. But Stockholm isn't in Norway, it's in Sweden. And you keep misspelling it. It's Stockholm, with a C. Not Stokholm.

JBLACK94710: Hello?

JBLACK94710: Hello?

NORTHGIRL999: I don't know what to say.

JBLACK94710: How can you not know what to say?

NORTHGIRL999: I just don't. Okay. So you found me out. Please don't hate me Jonah!

JBLACK94710: How can I hate you? I don't even know who you are!

NORTHGIRL999: Yes you do. Of course you know me. I'm someone you see all the time!

JBLACK94710: Who is this really?

NORTHGIRL999: Oh Jonah. I'm so embarrassed.

JBLACK94710: Don't be embarrassed. Just tell me who you are.

NORTHGIRL999: I can't believe you can't figure it out. Who do you think gave you the roses when you were in the hospital?

JBLACK94710: Cecily?

NORTHGIRL999: Oh Jonah it's so pathetic you think it was Cecily leaving you the roses.

JBLACK94710: I saw her leave my room!

NORTHGIRL999: Well, DUH, I mean of course she was there, there were lots of girls who visited you. But only one who left you roses.

JBLACK94710: PLEASE TELL ME WHO YOU ARE!!!!

JBLACK94710: Hello?

JBLACK94710: Hello?

JBLACK94710: Posie, that's not you, is it?

NORTHGIRL999: Oh, Jonah, it's not Posie. Don't you know?

JBLACK94710: How would I know who this is? Cecily?

NORTHGIRL999: Cold!

<u>JBLACK94710</u>: Cilla? Kirsten? Luna?

<u>NORTHGIRL999</u>: Cold! Freezing cold! You think I'm one of those dopey girls who sits around listening to Lemon?

<u>JBLACK94710</u>: Sophie?

<u>NORTHGIRL999</u>: Sophie? The girl from Masthead? Could you get any FURTHER from the truth?

<u>JBLACK94710</u>: Who are you?

<u>JBLACK94710</u>: Hello?

[Northgirl999 is not currently signed on.]

(Still Nov. 9, 11:45 P.M.)

I biked over to Posie's house today and she came to the door and said, "Hey, Jonah. What are the four sexiest words in the universe?"

"What?" I said.

And Posie said, "My parents aren't home."

We went inside and ran upstairs to her room, with the surfing pictures on the wall and the M. C. Escher mobile twirling from the ceiling above her desk, and started ripping each other's clothes off.

How can I describe what it's like to be going out with Posie after all these years? It's like doing all of my favorite things all at once. Like eating apple pie with toffee ice cream in bed and watching an *Indiana Jones* movie and having school cancelled on a Tuesday because of a hurricane. It's like listening to my favorite Smelts song played so loud it makes glasses shake in the kitchen cupboard. It's like laughing so hard I can't talk. It's like staying up all night and watching the sun turn the clouds red. It's like finding something totally new in something I've known my whole life. It's definitely cool.

So here's the bad part. I can't stand to even write it down. I mean, if there was a way to write this with my eyes closed, I'd do it. Posie and I were both naked and we'd been kissing and fooling around for like, twenty minutes, and I got up to go get one of the condoms out of my wallet. Super Fine Ribbed Extra Lubricated. And then, as I was opening the package I was looking at this picture of a racehorse Posie has on her wall, and it reminded me of Sophie. I guess it was that new leather smell that I associate with Sophie, like a baseball glove that's just been oiled. Her horses, and that house by the sea.

"Hey," Posie said, frowning at me. "Are you okay?"

"I'm fine," I said. Then Posie walked over and kissed my neck and took the condom out of my hand.

And at that second we heard the front door slam and Posie's mother yelled up the stairs "Posie? I'm home!"

Posie froze and called down the stairs, "Hi, Mom!"

We heard Mrs. Hoff's footsteps coming up the stairs and we pulled our clothes on in about five seconds. We didn't even bother with underwear, we just yanked on our pants and T-shirts and threw everything else under the bed. Then the door swung open.

"Guten Tag, Jonah Black," Posie's hefty Bavarian mother greeted me.

"Hello, Mrs. Hoff," I said.

She came into the room carrying a tray with a plate of cookies and two glasses of milk on it.

"I brought you zum koochen," she said, and put the cookies down on the bed. She looked around Posie's room, and wrinkled up her nose a little bit. Then she went over to the window and opened it wide.

"It smells a bit *unzeimlich* in here," she said. Then she turned and smiled. "It is so gut to see you, Jonah! You come over more often now, please?"

"Okay, Mrs. Hoff," I said, and she left the room.

Posie and I started laughing. We drank our milk.

Posie wiped the milk from her mouth with the back of her hand and smiled. "Better luck next time, Jonah," she said.

I knew what she meant by this. She wasn't

going to do it while her mom was downstairs. I didn't blame her. It did kind of spoil the mood.

"Hey, would you tell me something serious?" I said. "Are you Northgirl1999? On AOL?"

Posie looked at me without a clue. "Who?"

"Never mind," I said. "Forget it."

"No, seriously," she said. "Who's that?"

"Nobody," I said.

I'm about to go to bed. I'm drinking chocolate milk, which pretty much makes me an eight-year-old Cub Scout, but what can I tell you. I love to drink chocolate milk, and I love making it. I like putting the milk in first, which of course has to be real whole milk, not the gross skim milk Mom and Honey drink. Then I put in a spoon and I get the milk spinning around and around. When it's spinning good and fast I drizzle in the Bosco and watch the milk change color. It starts off white like snow then gets dirty, then beige, then finally it gets good and chocolaty and the question then is just how chocolaty can you get it before it'll taste disgusting? I mean, if it's too thin that's pretty bad, but if it's too chocolaty that's worse. You have to wait for it to stop spinning before you drink it. If you don't, you bruise the Bosco. It is kind of a science, I guess.

Most girls don't drink milk, I've noticed. I think they think it makes them fat. It's a shame girls can't enjoy food. It's like every time they eat something they have to work it into this complex matrix of How Much They've Exercised and How Many Calories This Has and all that junk. It's a shame. Especially since a milk mustache is like the sexiest thing in the universe. Not the ones in the "Got Milk" ad campaign, which always look like clumpy Elmer's Glue. Posie had this milk mustache the other day that was ridiculous, it was so sexy.

Anyway, all I'm saying is it's a shame more girls don't drink milk. It's good for you.

Nov. 12, 5:15 P.M.

So I saw Dr. LaRue today and it was amazing. All I did was talk about Posie. I spent most of the session telling him about our night out on the water. This was my favorite meeting with him so far. It was like reliving the whole night with her. I went over every single detail.

After that, we talked a little bit about Thorne. But I managed to get him back on the subject of Posie after a few minutes. I told him about almost sleeping with her that last time and how I saw that picture of the racehorse on Posie's wall and how it reminded me of Sophie.

And Dr. LaRue said, "Well, what about Sophie?"

"What about her?" I said.

"Do you still love her?" he said.

"That's a different kind of love," I said.

"How is it different?" Dr. La Rue said.

"With Sophie, it was the love of an idea, of being in love with someone who you're making this like, psychic bridge to, someone who's in trouble that you know you can save. It's like this perfect love, the love you have for music or the way a glass of ice water tastes on a hot day," I tried to explain.

"And how is that different from the way you feel about Posie?" Dr. LaRue asked me.

"Posie? Well, Posie's my friend. I've known her forever. With Posie it's like the way you love an old shirt that you've had so long it fits you perfectly because it knows the way your body goes," I said.

"You're saying Posie is like an old shirt?" Dr. LaRue laughed.

"I don't mean it that way. I mean I don't have to think about Posie and me fitting together; we just do."

"Which is the better love, Jonah?"

"Better?"

"Yes. You've said you have this love for the one girl, which is like an ideal, a perfect dream. And then you have this love for another girl, which is very tangible and familiar. I was wondering which love you think is the better kind," he said.

"I don't think you can compare the two," I said. "They're completely different."

"Is it the same emotion you feel, for both of them?" he said.

I wasn't sure where he was going with that. I mean I'd just finished telling him how different they were.

"No," I said, frowning. "I guess it's similar, in some ways—"

"But would you say you are in love with both of these girls?" he said.

"In love with both of them—I mean, yeah. Sort of," I answered, confused.

"Well, this is what strikes me as interesting, Jonah. Don't you see it as problematic that you're in love with two people at once?" he said.

"Yeah, but I just told you, it's different," I said.

"I understand that. But doesn't what you feel for Sophie somehow affect how you feel about Posie?" he said.

"I don't know. I mean, maybe," I stumbled.

"What I'm asking you, Jonah, is this. Whatever it was you felt about Sophie. Whatever it was that happened. What I want to know is, is it over?" Dr. LaRue said.

I was just about to tell him of course it's over, don't be stupid, but at that second I thought about her big house in Maine and I can see Sophie's horse walking along the sand by the ocean, but there is no one on it. I'm trying to imagine Sophie riding the horse, but I can't picture her. All I can see is Posie, her long, tan legs and her sunny face. And suddenly I have this terrible feeling that Sophie has disappeared. Where did she go?

I didn't answer Dr. LaRue's question. He looked at his watch and said, "Time's up."

(Still Nov. 12, later.)

When I got home, Posie was waiting for me. We sat on my bed and started to fool around, but we didn't get very far because Honey and Smacky were sitting out by the pool just outside the sliding glass door to my room, and my mother was out in the hallway doing yoga. Every few minutes she'd let out this long moan that is her mantra or something, and sounds like "vootie."

I got up and pulled the curtains on the glass door.

"You know, I think your sister and Smacky Platte are just about the weirdest couple in the universe," Posie said.

I nodded in complete agreement. "I think it's because he's the only one who isn't intimidated by her," I said.

———— ∎ ————

"Do you think he knows how smart she is, and he just doesn't care?" Posie asked me.

"No. I think he's just totally stupid," I said.

We both started laughing and then Mom knocked on the door. I opened it to find her wearing a brown unitard and holding a tray of cookies and milk.

How come our moms keep bringing us cookies all the time? Are they like, trying to keep us from having sex?

"Who likes Fudge Town?" Mom said, beaming happily at us. She was all mellowed out from her yoga.

We ate some cookies and then Posie had to head home. Honey and Smacky took off in Honey's Jeep, too, so it was just Mom and me in the house. After a while Mom came in to get the platter back and she sat on the edge of my bed. She was kind of glowing, like she was happy all over. I wondered if she was taking something.

"Mom?" I said. "Are you all right?"

"Oh, I am," Mom said. "I'm as happy as I've ever been."

"I'm glad. How come you're so happy?" I asked her.

"I'm happy about our family," she said. "I'm happy about my career. I'm happy about the way love can change people's lives."

"Mom," I said, totally embarrassed.

"Bup, bup, bup," Mom said, holding out her hand. "It's a truth we have to get comfortable with. Love has a transforming power. It changes us deep inside and makes us better people. Be glad for the changes love is making in our lives."

"Okay, Mom," I said, and I reached over and hugged her. It was corny, but I meant it. I knew what she meant.

Then her cell phone started ringing, and she stood up and checked her caller ID. "I have to take this," she said, and left the room.

As she went down the hall I heard her cooing into the phone. I don't think she was talking about love transforming my life or Honey's life. I think she was talking about herself. Mom has a boyfriend, I'm sure of it.

Nov. 13, 2:25 P.M.

I'm sitting here in Miss von Esse's class. Miss Tenuda's class was canceled because she's been absent for a few days. There's a rumor that she went crazy and quit her job and we're going to get a new teacher. It's pretty strange, the idea of your teacher losing her mind, although if I had to teach me I'd probably go crazy, too. I feel sorry for Miss Tenuda, though. I always liked her.

Miss von Esse is wearing a headband today and there's this one lock of hair that has fallen out of the headband and it's hanging around her face like one of those little mouthpieces that the telemarketers on TV always wear. *Can I take your order, please?* I can't figure out if she knows it's there and she's deliberately ignoring it, or if she's just oblivious. I can't imagine she'd be unaware of it because it keeps moving every time she does, which is a lot because Miss von Esse kind of dances while she teaches. We're learning the subjunctive case, which is a big deal in German because there are two different ways of saying it. It's like the Eskimos having ten different words for snow, or Honey having a hundred different names for me. The subjunctive is the way you talk when you're discussing things that aren't necessarily real right now, but they might be sooner or later. Like when you say If one thing, Then some other thing.

Actually, it's a pretty handy way of talking.

Like, If my neck continues to feel better, Then Mr. Davis might let me swim in the diving meet against Ely High. Or, If I get to dive in the meet, Then I will really make a fool of myself because I haven't even been in the water in like a month. Or, If Watches Boys Dive comes back from wherever she's been, Then I will feel glad and maybe try to show off some more for her.

Or, If I don't talk to Thorne pretty soon, Then maybe I'm never going to be friends with him again. Or, If Thorne were a normal person, Then I could be mad at him for screwing around with Luna behind Posie's back. But he's not so I can't. Or, If Thorne hadn't lied to me about being so rich, Then he wouldn't have been all embarrassed when I saw him working on the *Scrod*.

Miss von Esse hasn't said anything to me since I screwed up the German test. I got a C– on it, by the way. She just handed the test back and sighed. I think the worst feeling in the world is when you know you've disappointed someone.

Nov. 15, 6:35 P.M.

Posie sent off her college applications yesterday: University of Florida, University of Hawaii, University of California at Santa Cruz, Bowdoin, Wooster, and Kenyon. The three universities are basically recruiting her for surfing. The power of the Wahine! But Bowdoin, Wooster, and Kenyon don't even have an ocean, I don't think. If she decides to go to one of those, it's so she can become a student, like a real college girl. It's hard to imagine, but then again, Posie's smart. I mean, she's no Honor Elspeth Black, but she's smart.

It's kind of hard to watch the seniors all applying to college. I mean, I should be applying to college now, but I'm not. I'm still in eleventh grade studying James Buchanan, the bachelor president, who I happen to know went to Dickinson College, in Pennsylvania. How do I know this? Miss Tenuda told us, just before she flipped out. Actually, Miss Tenuda's flipping out is something I should have written about more. I mean, we were stuck on Zachary Taylor and Millard Fillmore and James Buchanan and Franklin Pierce for what seemed like all of October and half of November, but I don't think that means she was crazy like everyone is saying. Maybe she just wanted to avoid the Civil War. I can sympathize with that.

Anyway, now she's gone, and we have this new history teacher, Mr. Sadoff, and he's like some beatnik out of the 1950s. He's tall, with shaggy red hair and round John Lennon glasses, which he probably thinks is some kind of statement. He also has a goatee. Anyway, Mr. Sadoff immediately plunged us into the Civil War and he's making it pretty interesting, except that I already went through Gettysburg and Appomattox last year.

It's actually starting to get a little nippy in Florida, which is funny because in Pennsylvania right now the leaves are off the trees and everyone is walking around in down coats. Here it's just jean jackets and windbreakers, but it still feels like the year is coming to an end. Thanksgiving is next week, and I have to say I'm looking forward to it.

Posie is coming over to our house for dinner, and I am totally psyched. I'm thinking of inviting Thorne and his parents, too, just to be nice.

What else? Mr. Davis asked me how my head was and I said all better, and he wanted to know how I'd feel about diving with the team again, and I said I'd love to but I have to talk to my doctor first. Dr. Sheldon was not crazy about it. She said just because I feel better doesn't mean my head is all healed.

That struck me as the perfect explanation for the Posie/Sophie situation. I mean, I can say with good faith that I'm over Sophie and I'm completely in love with Posie, but I still think about Sophie every once in a while.

I'm still having trouble remembering what Sophie looks like, though. Which is probably a good thing.

I think that's all for now.

P.S. Honey is the only senior accepted early decision at Harvard. And the only one who applied.

This totally weird thing happened today after school when I was delivering pizzas for First Amendment. It was at the very end of my shift, and I was about to head home when Mr. Swede got this call for seven large pizzas to be sent to this house on 25th Ave., down by the cemetery. So I waited around and finally they were all boxed up and I had to use an extra bungee cord to make sure all the pizzas stayed on the bike. Anyway, I cycled along the streets, my head just kind of in the clouds. I was thinking about this one time I was sitting behind Sophie in geometry last year and she was drawing these doodles in the margin of her notebook. Sophie is a really good artist and she did the usual stuff, horses and flowers and curlicues and junk, but then she started drawing this girl, and I could tell right away it was a picture of herself. I mean, it was definitely Sophie, except she didn't have any eyes. And that was strange because Sophie's eyes are the most beautiful thing about her. But now I can't even remember what color her eyes are. Green, or blue?

Anyway, before I knew it I was at 25th Ave. and I rode past the cemetery, which is really creepy. It's not an old graveyard like the ones you see up in New England or something with old stone walls and tombstones dating back to the sixteen hundreds with vines growing all over them. This one has a kind of suburban blandness to it. All the grave-stones are small and new and look like they were just cut yesterday. The houses near the cemetery are all run-down, too. I mean they're fine, it's not a total slum or anything; they're just a little seedier than anything else in Pompano.

I pulled up at the house with the seven pizzas. The house I was delivering to was the worst house on the street. I mean there was a car up on blocks in the driveway and the screens were all torn and the grass was all rusty like it had never seen water. It wasn't the kind of place you'd think would order $82 worth of pizza, and I was thinking I probably wasn't going to get much of a tip.

———— ∎ ————

I rang the bell and waited, and nobody answered, so I rang the bell again and just stood there for what seemed like forever. Then I pushed the screen door open a little and called out, "Hello?"

Over the mantel in the den was this old stuffed marlin that seemed very familiar. And then I saw this picture on the wall of Thorne and his parents and I looked at the order slip and it said Wood. It was Thorne's house.

When the Woods moved here I don't even know, but it was really depressing. I walked into the house and called out, "Thorne?" but there was no answer.

Then I found Thorne's room. There was this huge computer sitting on his desk, and the floor was scattered with folders full of papers and pictures and a scanner and a laser printer and all this gear. There were all these ads for the Wood Love Rendezvous Connection. Suddenly I had this clear picture of what it's like to be Thorne. How he is constantly scheming and reinventing himself because he's trying to get the hell out of this house. It must be total torture to live in a place like Pompano where some people have mansions and yachts, and go to school at Don Shula with all the rich kids, and then come home to this.

On the desk were all his college applications.

There was one for Wesleyan and one for Amherst, and the University of Virginia, and Stanford. These were some of the best colleges in the country, and I know for a fact that Thorne doesn't have the SATs or the grades to get in. It was also weird that his applications were still here, because the college counselors at Don Shula made this big point of telling everybody to get them in by November 15th to show them you're serious. Maybe Thorne had finally found something he couldn't hustle.

Still, knowing Thorne, he'll find a way. If anybody can charm their way into college, Thorne can. Suddenly I really missed him. I felt bad seeing his house without him there. I wished I'd never known about this place or seen him on board the *Scrod*. I wished he'd told me about it himself, when he was ready.

And then I wondered, who in hell sent Thorne a huge pile of pizzas and try to stick him with the bill? For a second I thought it might be Posie, but she isn't mean enough for it. So who was it?

I was just about to get the hell out of there when I saw something that stopped me in my tracks. Thorne's room was a total mess, except for the top of his dresser, which was completely clean. It was the only place in the room that didn't look like a bomb had gone off. And on top of his dresser were three things. The first was this blue ribbon he'd gotten in track, back at Pompano Junior High. He'd won it like six years ago, but it was still there on top of his dresser, like a little ode to his youthful career as an athlete or something. And next to this was a framed photograph of Thorne and me standing in front of the ocean.

I remembered the day Posie took that picture. It was before I went up to Masthead, so it was at least two and a half years ago. We'd spent all day, Thorne and me, and Posie, hanging out on the beach. Posie was surfing, and Thorne and I were lying around drinking soda and listening to tunes on Thorne's box. It was a day pretty much like a million days Thorne and Posie and I spent together before I went up north, but just looking at the two of us smiling in the picture made life look like heaven. Thorne and I have our arms around each other's backs and these big goofy grins and we're squinting into the sun and we look totally contented. I guess that's why Thorne had it framed on his dresser; it was a perfect moment.

Next to the picture were the two pieces of my clamshell collar.

America Online Mail Center

To: <u>JBLACK94710</u>
From: <u>NORTHGIRL999</u>
Subject: Hungry?

Hey, Jonah. Did Thorne like his pizzas? Just wondering.
Actually I was thinking of maybe sending him one that was
half extra cheese, half snake.
Ha ha.

Love,
Northgirl999

P.S. Did you figure out who I am yet?

—— ■ ——

I've got a lot to write about tonight.

I was on my way home from my route for First Amendment, when I biked past the Wimpy's on Federal Highway. It's this really gross place next to the head shop and the topless bar, and it has this big sign: HOT DOGS 3 FOR $1. And I saw Thorne standing in line.

I pulled over and locked the bike and got in line, but Thorne didn't see me. So then I just sort of casually said, "Hey, I hear the food here is really good."

Thorne turned around. "Jonah!" he said. I could tell his brain was working a million miles an hour trying to figure out how to finesse the situation, but he knew I was onto him.

"It's okay, Thorne," I said. "I don't give a damn. I really don't."

"Yeah, well, I do," Thorne said. He reached the window and he gave the man a buck and got his three hot dogs. The man looked at me and I gave him a buck and then Thorne and I sat down at a beat-up picnic table to eat our lame-o hot dogs, watching the traffic.

"Listen, it's okay about Posie," Thorne said. "I screwed up with her, okay? I should never have tried to nail her in the first place."

"Yeah, well. I'm sorry I was so pissed off at you about her, but you know how I feel about Posie. She's not like other girls," I said.

"So are you like, totally grooving on her now?" he asked me.

I shrugged. "She's pretty awesome," I said.

"Well, if you feel that way it's a good thing it's you instead of me," said Thorne. "Really. You're much more of a . . . whatever."

"Yeah?" I said. "Thanks."

"I'm just sorry I . . ." Thorne started to say, but he couldn't finish it.

I knew what he wanted to tell me. He was sorry he'd lied to me.

"Thorne," I said. "You know I don't care about how much money you have. Do you really think that makes a difference to me?"

"Well, it makes a difference to me, goddammit.

Ever since the motel went out of business, it's been pretty crappy at home. My parents don't have money for anything anymore. Mom is working for the Chamber of Commerce, answering phones, plus she does people's laundry and ironing. Dad wakes up at three o'clock every morning to take his crappy fishing boat out, and I have to help him every weekend. They have just enough to pay the bills and keep the fridge full of Velveeta and cornflakes. It totally sucks."

"Yeah, well. I'm still your friend, Thorne," I said quietly.

"Yeah?" he said. He sounded totally surprised. "How come?"

"What can I tell you?" I said. "You've got character."

Thorne looked at his hot dog like he was wondering what kind of meat was in it. "Yeah, I got character all right."

"You do," I said. "Just do me a favor? Don't pretend to be calling your broker on your cell phone, okay? It's obnoxious."

"Who? You mean Kendra?" he said.

"Yeah. You don't have to do that anymore," I told him.

"Hey, man, Kendra's real," Thorne said. "You should see this chick. Dreadlocks to her waist! I thought having her do some transactions for me might give her a more personal interest in my *portfolio*."

"Did it work?"

Thorne nodded. "The market's definitely up," he said.

I just shook my head. "You're insane," I said.

"Hey, Jonah," said Thorne. "You remember when I got you Sophie's phone number, and you said you'd tell me what happened with her? You never did tell me the story."

"I know," I said.

"How come?" Thorne said.

"I don't know. I guess I was afraid you'd think I was a loser," I said.

"Well, if you're a loser maybe you and me got something in common," Thorne said, clapping me on the back.

"You really want to hear it?" I said.

"Yeah. I think I do. It's better than eating these monkey-meat hot dogs, anyway," he said.

"All right," I said. "I'll tell you."

And I started to tell Thorne the story about Sophie, the whole story. It was the first time I'd told anybody. And now that I've told him, I don't even know why I was keeping it such a big secret. I guess I just felt stupid about it. I still do.

I'm going to try to write it down now. It may not

be exactly the way I said it to Thorne, but it'll be close enough.

But first I'm going to get a drink. I need my strength.

Okay. I'm back. Here's what happened.

THE TRUE STORY OF SOPHIE O'BRIEN, MASTHEAD ACADEMY, AND HOW I LOST MY DRIVER'S LICENSE. BY MR. JONAH BLACK.

Once upon a time there was a boy named Jonah whose parents got divorced. After the divorce, Jonah's father decided it would be good if Jonah spent some time closer to where he lived so he arranged it so that Jonah would leave his home in Pompano Beach, Florida, and begin attending Masthead Academy in Bryn Mawr, Pennsylvania, which was only about five minutes from Dad's house. Masthead was a boarding school and even though Jonah's father only lived about five minutes away, Jonah almost never saw Dad. When he did, Dad always sort of acted like he wished Jonah wasn't there, especially since Dad had married his twenty-three-year-old secretary named Tiffany. When Tiffany was around Dad didn't pay much attention to anything else, and Tiffany was always around.

I think I have to stop writing it this way because it already sounds too awful.

And it wasn't all awful. It was kind of interesting to be going to school at Masthead. The teachers were all really smart, and it was cool to be going to such a good school. Most of the students were incredibly wealthy. It was like they had no idea there was anybody in the world who didn't have as much stuff as they did. Or maybe they knew that such people existed, but they just weren't interested in them.

Anyway, Sophie O'Brien was this beautiful girl. Kind of frail, kind of distant, and really artistic. She didn't really hang out with anybody, and she seemed incredibly private. I used to see her in the art studio sometimes when no one else was there, painting these huge canvases. She had a completely unique view of the world, you could tell from her paintings. But I also always felt like something terrible had happened to her, or maybe she felt like something terrible was about to happen to her. She would paint things like a girl jumping off a cliff, or a train bearing down on someone sleeping on the tracks. One time she drew this bull's-eye with all these arrows headed toward it. She called it *Self-Portrait*.

—— ■ ——

My roommate at Masthead was this heinous guy called Sullivan. If I had a photograph of him, I'd paste it in here, because words don't exactly do him justice. People called him Sullivan the Giant, which was not exactly a compliment. I found out later his father was one of the trustees, which is the only explanation for why he was there, because he never cracked a book and barely went to class. He loved to eat and he'd eat these Italian subs every day that were the size of firewood, and then he'd fart these awful farts all night while he was sleeping. He was pretty disgusting, and he thought his disgustingness was just great. It gave him a lot of pleasure. In fact he'd brag about it.

We used to lie in our beds in the dorm room and he'd tell me everything he'd done to whatever girl he'd seen that night. He was always with some girl, which I did not understand at all, until he explained how he had all their files and records and he would do stuff like get them expelled or expose something they wanted kept secret unless they slept with him. It made me sick to see how proud he was for being such a monster. Sullivan always took his girls down to this seedy motel called the Beeswax Inn. Not that you were allowed to leave campus or anything, but the proctors always looked the other way when it came to Sullivan because he had dirt on them, too. He was a real slimeball, Sullivan the Giant.

Sullivan developed this plan to sleep with every single girl in the junior class, and he started going through them all in alphabetical order. Sophie's last name is O'Brien, and it took him until May to get that far down on the list. Knowing about Sullivan's plan gave me the creeps, but when Sophie's turn came, I really freaked out. It suddenly struck me that the terrible thing that was going to happen to her, the thing she was painting when she did that bull's-eye, was called Sullivan.

One day I saw Sophie in the gym. She was in the gymnastics room, all by herself, hanging from the rings. She was a pretty good gymnast, although she didn't join the team. She just went in there every once in a while and swung around on the rings and the parallel bars. Anyway, I stood up in the gallery and watched her through the window and it was pretty obvious she had no idea what was about to happen to her. I mean, if she did, she wouldn't have spent so much time alone, and like, made herself look so vulnerable and available. She was the perfect target for someone like Sullivan.

Suddenly I got this idea. I was going to save her. I knew what Sullivan had done to all the other girls, and how he treated them afterward. But not this time. I wasn't going to let him ruin Sophie.

There was this end-of-the-year formal dance at Masthead. Sullivan's plan was to take Sophie to the dance, and afterward he'd bring her to the Beeswax Inn, where I guess there was some sort of understanding that kids from Masthead could go to have sex without the management calling the administration. I even knew what room he was going to be in. There was this one special room called the Beehive Suite, which was on the ground floor and had a fireplace and a bay window. Sullivan had decided to spend the extra thirty dollars so he could deflower Sophie in the Beehive Suite. As if that would make things better.

The problem was, I didn't know how to stop Sullivan. I wanted to go up to Sophie and tell her what a loser he was, but (this is the horrible thing I don't want to write down) I was too shy to talk to her. I don't think Sophie O'Brien even knew I was alive.

I asked this girl Betsy Donnelly to the formal. I didn't really know her, but we were in the same world literature class with Mr. Fontaine, who everybody called Egg with Glasses. He had this big bald head and everything.

When I went to Betsy's dorm room to walk her over to the dance, she looked really pretty. She had on a long black dress, and her brown hair hung down almost to her waist. She was short, with little freckles all over her face, and she was wearing this black headband, which you'd think would look nerdy, but on Betsy it looked nice. I felt kind of bad about taking her to the dance just so I could look out for Sophie, but Betsy was smart. I guess you have to be smart if you go to Masthead. Unless you're Sullivan.

Anyway, as we were walking over to the dance, we had this bizarre conversation. Betsy had her hand resting on the crook of my arm. It was all very formal, like something out of Victorian England or something.

Halfway to the Great Hall where the dance was going to be, Betsy said, "Listen, Jonah, I know I'm not your first choice for the dance. But thanks for asking me. I wouldn't have gone if you didn't ask me."

"What?" I said, all nervous. "Who said you're not my first choice?"

"Jonah, let's be real, okay? Tonight's going to be fun. I just don't want to pretend this is like a date, though, all right?" she said.

"Well, I want it to be fun," I said. I appreciated the fact that she was being honest, but I was also embarrassed.

"I know you're up to something," she said. "I just don't know what exactly."

"Up to something?" I said. "What am I up to?"

"You're trying to stop him," she said, very quietly.

I opened my mouth to say something, but I didn't know what to tell her. So finally I just said, "You think I can?"

"I don't know," she said. "But I wish you would. Everyone wishes you would. At least those of us in the first half of the alphabet."

I thought about this, and then I got this kind of sick feeling.

"You mean he . . ." I started to say, staring at Betsy.

She kind of pulled into herself, like a turtle. "I just wish you'd stop him. He's a creep. Sophie doesn't deserve to have it be like that."

"Listen, can I ask you something? Why doesn't she just say no to him? Why doesn't everyone just say no?" I said.

She shrugged. "He's very persuasive," she said. "He knows stuff about you. He finds things out. It's really psycho, the way he works. It's horrible."

"Then why doesn't someone tell Mr. Plank?" I said. Mr. Plank was our headmaster.

"You think people haven't?" she said.

We were getting near the Great Hall now.

"Listen," Betsy said. "You do what you have to do. I just wanted to say I'm glad you asked me to the dance. It's nice to go with you, okay?"

"Okay," I said.

So we walked into the dance and we danced and stood around and drank fruit punch and then we danced some more. The band was this group of really old guys called The Secret Life. It was like dancing to a band with your grandparents playing in it.

While I was dancing, I wished that I liked Betsy more than I did, because she was really a cool girl.

Sullivan the Giant and Sophie were dancing, and if a song was at all slow, he'd hold her close to him and grope her. It looked like he was eating her or something, it was horrible. Everyone was looking at them, and a lot of the girls were looking at Sophie with this expression of total pity, especially the ones whose last names were in the first half of the alphabet. The guys, meanwhile, were all just looking at Sullivan like he was the greatest lover in the universe and they wished they knew his secret. It made me sick to my stomach.

At one point, while the band was taking a break, Betsy came up to me and said urgently, "Listen. Mr. Stubbs took his coat off."

I stared at her, and for a second it seemed like her freckles were blinking on and off, like Christmas lights.

"Yeah?" I said. I wasn't sure why I should care about Mr. Stubbs' coat.

"You know how he has that Peugeot?" Betsy said.

"Yeah." Actually, everyone knew about Mr. Stubbs' Peugeot. It sat in front of Zlatin Hall all day like a tourist attraction. It was this sleek, new silver car. Mr. Stubbs polished it every single weekend. It would be hard for anybody not to know about it.

Betsy hugged me suddenly, and it felt good to feel her arms around me. Then she pressed something into my hand, and I looked down and there was this car key and an emblem on the ring that said: PEUGOT.

The band started playing again, and I put the key in my pocket, and we started dancing again. A plan started taking shape in my head. I knew Sullivan would be taking Sophie to the Beeswax Inn, which sits on a bluff overlooking the Schuylkill River. It was just a matter of time.

I saw Sophie and Sullivan leaving the dance. Betsy gave me another hug. "Good luck, Jonah," she said.

I followed them out of the Great Hall. When I got outside, Sophie was leaning against a wall, waiting for Sullivan to come and get her. She was wearing a navy-blue dress and lipstick so dark red it was almost black. I wanted to say, "Don't do it, Sophie," and grab her hand and run away with her to safety. But then Sullivan pulled up in his Saab, and opened the door. Sophie hesitated for just a second, and then she stepped into Sullivan's car and they drove away.

Mr. Stubbs' Peugeot was down a little hill in the parking lot between the gym and Zlatin Hall. I ran over to it, and the next thing I knew I was on my way to the Beeswax Inn.

I'm not sure I knew exactly what I was going to do once I got there. I think I had some idea of bursting into the Beehive Suite and yelling at Sullivan and picking Sophie up in my arms and carrying her to safety. But since I hadn't even had the courage to talk to Sophie before this, I'm not sure that I could have done that. Maybe I could have gone up to the front desk and told them something was wrong in the Beehive Suite, and had them send in the cops or something. Maybe I would have gotten there and just sat in the parking lot, unable to do anything but sit there like a loser.

In fact, if I hadn't had the accident, that's probably exactly what would have happened.

Except that I did have the accident. It's not that hard to explain it, actually. As I pulled into the parking lot, I saw two shadows against the curtains in the Beehive Suite and instead of hitting the brake I must have stepped on the gas. I plowed Mr. Stubbs'

Peugot straight through the bay window and the next thing I knew glass was breaking and the air bag in the car was inflating and people were screaming and the horn of the Peugot went off and wouldn't stop.

There was a brief period of time between when I drove the car through the window and when the cops showed up. For some reason, I didn't have a scratch on me, unlike the Peugot, which was totaled, so I got out of the car and walked through the hole in the wall, into the Beehive Suite. The door to the room was standing open, and on the bed was Sophie's purse, and a bra.

I could hear people yelling and I knew there was about thirty seconds left before people started pouring into the room. If they found Sophie's purse they'd realize she'd been there, and Sophie would get connected to this whole disaster which was now, somehow, my fault.

So I grabbed her purse and I stuffed the bra into my pocket and then I ran outside and threw the purse into the Schuylkill River. I heard the splash.

Then a cop car drove up and two cops got out. They surveyed the situation and shone a flashlight in my face and said, "Is this your car, son?"

As I heard myself saying, "No," I realized for the first time exactly how much trouble I was in.

Mr. Stubbs was a real sport about the whole thing.

He didn't press charges for auto theft, although Dad did have to pay a huge insurance bill. Also Mr. Stubbs made sure I was expelled from Masthead, and I was forbidden to ever set foot on the property again. Plus, I had my license revoked by the police. Oh, and Dad also had to pay the Beeswax Inn for repairs, not to mention the $59.99 it turned out I owed them for the room because Sullivan, on top of everything else, had rented out the room in my name. I guess he thought it would be funny.

Speaking of funny, they also found the bra in my pocket, which is why my mother was convinced that I had some sort of issue with girls' underwear. That's partly why she insisted I go see Dr. LaRue after I got back to Pompano.

None of these disasters especially mattered to me, though, because the last thing I saw before I got hauled off in the cop car that night, was Sophie O'Brien running down the street, still wearing her navy-blue dress, while Sullivan stood on the corner yelling at her to get back in his car. She'd escaped! As the cops drove me past I looked at Sophie and she looked back at me and for just that instant she seemed to be thinking, *Hey, I know you.*

All right, so this is what I told Thorne, more or less. We sat by Federal Highway for a long time.

Thorne didn't finish his hot dogs. Finally he said to me, "And she doesn't know what you did for her?"

"I don't know what she knows," I said. "I got thrown out of there that night. I haven't been back."

"Why don't you call her then, and tell her what you did? You're like, her hero, man," he said.

"She doesn't even know who I am," I said.

"You think?"

"Anyway, if I was too chicken to talk to her before the night of the dance, you think there's any way I'm going to be able to talk to her now?"

Thorne suddenly got this weird look on his face. "You know what, Jonah? Your worries are over."

"What do you mean?" I said.

"You leave it to me. I got an idea," Thorne said.

"I don't want to leave it to you. I don't want you to have an idea," I pleaded, beginning to panic. I could tell Thorne was cooking up one of his schemes.

"C'mon. I owe ya," Thorne said, and he stood up. "You just have to trust me."

I looked at Thorne, and knowing what I know about him, those were some of the funniest words I'd ever heard him say. But me and Thorne have been friends forever and ever, and after today I felt like maybe we'd risen to a new level of friendship or something. Anyway, at that second, I did trust him.

"Okay," I said.

Nov. 18, 6 P.M.

Posie was competing in the Pompano Triple-A Meet, and there was a big crowd of people out on the dune, watching. I felt so proud, standing on the beach, watching her surf. Every time I see her, I can't believe she's actually that perfect. Posie gives the whole universe a sense of balance when she surfs.

I climbed up on the lifeguard tower to watch her, and I got a little sad. I was thinking about how Posie's going to graduate pretty soon, and then she'll probably be leaving, either to go to college or maybe to surf the pro circuit. Either way, I'll get left behind. Stuck in Mr. Bond's homeroom at Don Shula. That is, assuming I ever become a senior.

———— ■ ————

While I was up there, Pops Berman climbed up the tower and sat down next to me. It's amazing how Pops always magically appears when I'm there. It's like he's enchanted or something.

Pops hacked into his fist and pounded on his chest.

"Are you okay?" I asked him.

"I got a chest full a mucus," he said, and spat. "I'm fine." He looked over at me. "How you doin', Chipper?"

"I'm good."

"You get over that dream girl now that you got a real one?" Pops said.

"Yeah," I said. "I guess."

Pops looked down at his feet and sighed loudly. Actually it was more like a growl. "Oh, no," he said. "No, you don't."

"What?" I said.

"You're not over her. I can't believe it. And here I was so sure you'd stopped being a lunkhead," he gasped, wheezing.

"I'm over her. All right? I'm over her," I said, trying to sound more sure of myself this time.

"You're not. Something's happened. Come on, Chipper, let's hear it. What's the story?"

"There's no story. I've just been thinking about her recently. Yesterday I told my friend Thorne about what happened with Sophie at boarding school, and it's the first time I've ever really told someone the whole truth. I guess it just stirred some things up, that's all," I told him.

"You see that girl?" Pops said, pointing at Posie with his cane. She was walking through the surf carrying her board under one arm. She looked like some kind of sea goddess.

"Yeah."

"Now you treat that girl nice, you love her like there's no tomorrow, and you concentrate on the job at hand, Chipper. You don't have any reason to stir anything up. You treat that girl like she's an angel. Or so help me God I'm going to whack you on the head," he said, gasping for breath.

He coughed into his fist and then he started climbing down the tower.

"Pops, where you going?" I said.

"I'm going home. I'm too angry," he snarled.

"Pops—"

"Shut up, Chipper," he said, storming off. "You've got me all pissed off now."

Sophie comes riding out of the ocean and up to the tower on her horse. She slides off the horse and climbs up the ladder and I think, *Oh, yeah, that's what she looks like*. Her face is clearer than ever. I can see the sun reflecting off the ocean spray in her hair and she sits down next to me and kisses me softly, her emerald-green eyes shining. She looks out at Posie, who is riding a big wave, and says, "Hey, Jonah, who's that?" but at that exact second I can't remember Posie's name.

Nov. 19, 4:30 P.M.

When I got home from school today, I saw the weirdest thing. Thorne's car was pulling out of the driveway.

I thought maybe this was part of Thorne's Big Plan, whatever that was. But all I could imagine was that Thorne was trying to sleep with my sister. Or my mother. I don't know which one would be more disgusting.

When I got inside, I said, "Mom, what was Thorne doing here?" and she looked at me like I was crazy. "Thorne? Your friend Thorne Wood? Thorne wasn't here, sweetie."

"Okay, fine, whatever," I said.

But then Mom said, "Jonah, would you sit down? We need to talk."

Oh, no, I thought.

"Sure, Mom," I said. "What's on your mind?"

"I wanted to ask you something," she said.

"Go ahead," I said.

"Well, what I want to know is, do you believe in love, Jonah?" She cocked her head to one side like a basset hound.

"Love?" I said. I felt like this must be a trick question, but I wasn't sure.

"Yes," Mom said.

"Do I believe in love?" I repeated.

"Yes."

"Yes, I do, Mom," I said. "Sure I do."

"I'm so glad! I've often worried that you'd find it hard to believe in love, after your father and I separated," she said.

"No. I still believe in it," I assured her.

"Well, good," she said. Then she got up. She put some water in a teapot and got out a bag of chamomile tea.

"Was that everything you wanted to ask me?" I said.

"Yes, Jonah," she said. "That's all."

I left the kitchen and went back to my room. I didn't feel very good about our conversation. It seemed like my mother and I had reached some sort of agreement, but I wasn't sure what we'd agreed on.

My door swung open and Honey was standing there. "I vant to suck your blood," she said.

"Hi, Honey," I said.

She sat down on my desk. "Guess you and Ma had a little talk, huh?" she said.

"Yeah, what is this all about anyway? Has she been talking to Mrs. Hoff?" I said.

"What? You think this is about you?" my sister said.

"It's not about me?" I said, surprised.

"Since when has Mom ever thought about either of us?" Honey said.

"That's not fair. She thinks about us," I said.

"Clamface, Ma's in love. Can't you tell? She's trying to break us in. She's bringing somebody to Thanksgiving dinner," Honey said, like it was the most obvious thing in the world.

"Ma? In love?"

Honey nodded. "That's my theory."

"Jesus," I said. Honey's theories were usually pretty accurate.

"So what do you think? Are you all right with it?" she asked me.

"With Mom being in love? I guess. Depends on with who," I said.

"Well, aren't you open-minded. You want to know my opinion? Screw him. Whoever it is. Tell him to take a hike. I'm not cooperating," she said.

"Well, it looks like you've got it all figured out," I said.

"Exactly." She lifted her legs out in front of her and looked at them. They were still pretty pale. "Listen, Frankenstein. I was thinking maybe you're right about Smacky," she said. "Him being a potential prison convict and everything. Maybe I should set my sights a little higher."

"Honey, please tell me you're not going out with Thorne. Just tell me that," I said.

Honey looked like she was about to gag. "Thorne? You mean your sleazeball friend? Puh-lease, Jonah. I mean really."

Now I was convinced I was insane. Maybe the car I'd seen wasn't Thorne's. Maybe it was just someone who'd been idling in front of the house, checking a map or something.

"Anyway, I just wanted you to know," Honey said. "In case you see Smacky around. He's taking it pretty rough. My breaking up with him, I mean."

"He is? How do you mean?" I said.

"He's going to join the Air Force," Honey said.

I laughed. "Wow. You know what, Honey? You're all right," I said. "Sometimes I can actually stand you."

"I won't tell anyone," she said. And then she left.

NORTHGIRL999: Hello Jonah!

JBLACK94710: You know what? I think I know who you are!

NORTHGIRL999: You'll never guess.

JBLACK94710: You're Watches Boys Dive, aren't you?

NORTHGIRL999: ???????

JBLACK94710: You're the girl with the long black hair that comes to all the diving meets and watches me dive. I call you Watches Boys Dive because you look Indian.

NORTHGIRL999: You mean the chick with the waist-length black hair?

JBLACK94710: YES!!!

NORTHGIRL999: Who goes to St. Winnifreds?

JBLACK94710: I don't know where she goes to school.

NORTHGIRL999: Wears lots of turquoise jewelry?

JBLACK94710: YES! YES!

NORTHGIRL999: Sorry Jonah. I ain't her either.

JBLACK94710: Then how do you know so much about her?

NORTHGIRL999: Oh Jonah, everyone's seen her. She's another one of your adoring fans.

JBLACK94710: You've seen her?

NORTHGIRL999: Of course. If you go to any of the diving team practices, you always see her.

JBLACK94710: Wait. You've come to watch me practice? You've sat right there in the stands?

NORTHGIRL999: Of course.

JBLACK94710: Um. I guess it's a little embarrassing that I still don't know who you are.

NORTHGIRL999: It's more than embarrassing. It proves my point exactly. You don't SEE people Jonah. You look right through them. All you see is like your own little fantasy world.

JBLACK94710: I don't know. Maybe that used to be true. But I think I'm looking at things differently now. I think I'm more into what is real now.

NORTHGIRL999: Why? Because you're in love with Posie now?

JBLACK94710: Well, yeah. A little bit. I mean, that changes the way I see things.

NORTHGIRL999: And you really think you're over Sophie? Just because you're in love with Posie now? Boy, you're pathetic.

JBLACK94710: IS THERE ANYTHING ABOUT ME THAT YOU DON'T KNOW????????

NORTHGIRL999: I don't think so.

JBLACK94710: Mom? Honey? Miss von Esse? Mrs. Perella?

NORTHGIRL999: Don't be stupid. You think any of those people know you as well as I do?

JBLACK94710: Thorne? Posie???????

NORTHGIRL999: LOL!!! ROTFLMAO!!!!! You really don't have a clue, do you?

JBLACK94710: WHO IS THIS? PLEASE TELL ME!!! I'LL DO ANYTHING IF YOU'LL JUST TELL ME WHO YOU ARE!!!

JBLACK94710: Hello?

[Northgirl999 is not currently signed on.]

Today was kind of a momentous day, for a couple of reasons. First, it was my first day back in the water with the swim team. I only did a couple of dives, nothing too ambitious, but I did them well and it felt great. My head feels fine. Mr. Davis tried not to make a big deal out of it, but he was definitely watching me carefully to see how I was doing. I was totally psyched. I think I've missed diving a lot more than I realize.

We have a big meet against Ft. Lauderdale tomorrow, and it's not clear if Mr. Davis is going to let me dive in it or not. I know he needs me because Wailer and Ricky are still pretty lame, but he also doesn't want to rush me. It's all I can do not to get down on my knees and beg him to let me compete. But I'm trying to just accept whatever comes.

The second thing that happened to me today was this weird moment I had with Mr. Bond, the senior class homeroom teacher. I was on my way out of Sadoff's class after yet another agonizing day of the Civil War, and Mr. Bond stopped me in the hallway.

"Jonah Black," he said. "How are you enjoying American history? Do you like it?"

"Yeah," I said. "It's okay. I studied it all last year, though."

"Yes. Yes, I'd heard that," he said. He pushed those black glasses he wears up on his nose. "Well, what about the Civil War?"

"It's okay," I said. I really couldn't figure out why he was talking to me.

Mr. Bond ran his hands through his gelled hair, and his eyes lit up like he'd just had an idea. "There's a lot to learn from the Civil War," he said, looking excited. "Take the Battle of Cold Harbor, for instance, or Grant in the Wilderness. You know what Grant did, Jonah? He just kept sending in more troops. No matter how many of his men got slaughtered. He just kept pressing his advantage, refusing to give up."

I nodded. "Yeah, I remember that," I said.

"Well," said Mr. Bond. "You take care now."

I walked away, wondering if Mr. Bond had lost his mind. Maybe there was some kind of epidemic going around. First Miss Tenuda and now Mr. Bond.

The third thing that happened today was I saw Thorne after practice. He was leaning against a car, making out with Donna Mannocchi, who I've always been kind of fascinated with because she brings her own grated cheese to school every day to sprinkle on her lunch. Thorne whispered something in Donna's ear, and she jumped into her car and drove off. Then Thorne just stood there, waiting for me to walk up to him.

"Hey," I said.

"Hey, Jonah," he said.

"So you're with Donna Mannocchi now?" I said. "Man, you're amazing."

"What's amazing?" Thorne said.

"It's like you're never satisfied," I said.

"Satisfied? Of course I'm satisfied! You know, that's one of the things I don't understand about you, man. When you fall for a girl it's like one of those trapdoors in a gladiator movie or something, it's like one minute you're standing in front of somebody and the next minute you're falling into the pit where all the alligators are," Thorne said.

"Is that good, or bad?" I asked him.

"No, it's good," he said. "You're lucky. I never

feel that way about a chick, ever. I mean, to me they're all like Disney World or something. Like one girl is Pirates of the Caribbean, and another one is Space Mountain and some other chick is like, The Bear County Jamboree."

"That's beautiful, man," I said.

"I'm serious. It's like, I can't imagine going to Disney World and just riding the Haunted House again and again and again, like, never going on any of the other rides all day, just because I like the Haunted House," Thorne said. "I'd go nuts!"

"I think I'm losing you," I said.

"I know you are, man," said Thorne. "That's 'cause chicks aren't like Disney World to you. They're like, some whole other thing."

"I like to think of them as humans," I said.

"Just like you," Thorne said.

"Humans, but not just like me," I said, smiling.

Thorne shook his head. "What can I tell you, Jonah. You've got a philosophy, I guess."

"So do you, Thorne," I said, and he laughed.

"Hey, can I ask you a question? Honestly? Were you at my house yesterday afternoon?" I asked him.

"Yesterday? No way, man," Thorne said. "I was down by the dune with Elanor Brubaker. Why? Did someone say I'd been there?"

"Nah. Forget it," I said.

"Okay. Whatever," he said.

Posie's parents are going away again at Thanksgiving, and she and I are hatching a plan. She's having Thanksgiving dinner with me at my house. And afterward we're going to go over to her place and do it. Finally!

I'm not sure exactly how I feel about this. Of course I'm completely happy about it, I'm more than happy. I mean, come on—sex with Posie! But I'm anxious, too. I want it to be the best thing that's ever happened to us. I want it to be the most perfect, amazing experience of our lives. But if it is, *then* what? Is it all downhill from there? And if it *isn't*, then maybe we shouldn't do it. I mean, I don't want to ruin what we already have.

But none of this is enough to stop me from going ahead with it. No way.

I guess it's like Honey always says, "You never know until you try it." And I definitely want to try it.

Nov. 21, 8 P.M.

The end of a pretty amazing day.

Today we only had a half a day of school because of Thanksgiving. But in the afternoon was the Broward All-County Swim Meet, and Mr. Davis asked me to get suited up and sit with the team. Before the meet started he asked me if I was willing to dive and I said I thought so but I wasn't sure. I mean it's not like I've practiced much in the last month.

Anyway, we were competing against two other teams—Ft. Lauderdale Episcopal and Ely High. Episcopal's diving team was even more pathetic than ours, if that's possible, although it's not because they weren't talented. It's just that their divers were incredibly nervous and made some very basic errors, like this one guy who didn't have enough of his foot off the board before starting a back somersault so he dove like he'd fallen out of an airplane. I would have laughed except that the last time I was in an official meet I wound up in the hospital, so look who's talking?

Wailer and Ricky were hanging in there, doing their best. And Martino Suarez did his one-and-a-half somersault.

Eventually it came down to us and Ely High, and I have to say, those guys are really good. They have this one guy named Lamar Jameson who looks like some sort of statue. He's about six three, black, a shaved head, and his whole body is like one solid muscle. Anyway, Lamar was doing these killer dives, including a couple of amazing Division II dives that pretty much left everybody else in the dirt. But Ely had these three other guys who are not in Lamar's league, and they made some basic mistakes, too, although they weren't as pathetic as Episcopal.

Amazingly enough, Wailer did some very good dives. He pulled off a one-and-a-half somersault with a twist that was like a perfect textbook dive. Everybody went nuts, because the main thing Wailer is known for is falling off the board like a cement mixer. And Ricky Anderson was doing very well, too, although after every dive he always did the breaststroke to the ladder and it was so obvious that he wanted everyone to notice that he's this championship breaststroker and not to judge him from his diving which he's only doing because Mr. Davis forced him to.

So there we were, and the stands were packed. A lot of people I know were in the stands, which is funny because you'd think most people would be off enjoying the break. Posie was there, and next to her were my mom and Honey. I wondered if maybe Posie got them to come to cheer me on, which was nice, except the only thing I was doing was sitting on the bench.

At least this was true until Mr. Davis came over to me and asked if I wanted to give it a try. And I said, "Definitely."

I walked up to the high board and the PA system announced, "Jonah Black, Don Shula." And everybody cheered. I mean they were stamping their feet on the floor and clapping like I was all the members of 'N Sync in one body. I climbed up the ladder and I heard this voice shout, "Come on, Chipper!" Even though I couldn't see him I thought, *Whoa, even Pops Berman is here.*

Suddenly, I looked over at the bleachers, which I knew was going to piss off Mr. Davis, but I had to look. And there she was, Watches Boys Dive! She was sitting in her old spot by the window at the top of the bleachers. Her long black hair flowed down to her lap, and she was wearing a turquoise bead necklace. She looked at me and smiled.

Again, Mr. Davis had signed me up for a simple dive, a one-and-a-half somersault with a twist. But I decided to try the Division I dive that I nearly killed myself doing last time.

You'd think that this would be the stupidest idea I could possibly have had, and maybe it was. But somehow, standing up there I felt completely confident. I looked over at Posie, and I knew I could do it. The back two-and-a-half somersault with a one-and-a-half twist. Famous last words.

So I stood at the end of the board, with my back to the water, balancing on the balls of my feet with my heels sticking out over the edge. And I let all my thoughts drain completely out of me until I felt like an erased blackboard. Then I pressed down on the board with all my strength and raised my hands straight up like I was going to touch the lights on the ceiling. Then I bounced once, twice, three times off the board and I was flying.

Without thinking I did the somersaults, one, two, two and a half, still gaining height, and then, right at the top of my dive this bizarre thing happened.

I guess I should have known what was going to

happen because it was exactly what happened to me last time. I thought about Sophie.

I had this visual image of myself starting to fall, tumbling through the air, my head whacking the board, and me falling into the water again. The ride to the hospital in the paramedic's van. Spending the next day drifting in and out of dreams. I imagined Sophie on the beach, riding her horse, and I can see her hair blowing in the breeze off the ocean and I say to her, "Sophie, what are you doing here?" And she says, "Shush, Jonah," and covers my mouth with her hand. I can taste her fingers and they taste like crayons.

I kiss her one last time and she hugs me and I start to talk again but she just says, "Shush. You don't have to explain. I understand. I just want to say thank you, Jonah. You're a good man." And I think *man*? I'm just a guy, but I think I know what she means.

"Good-bye, Jonah," she says, and she walks off down the beach and it's all right. I'm not going to follow her.

I started to fall and I did the twists and I tucked my head in perfectly and then, with barely a splash, I sliced into the water. I'd done it. The two-and-a-half somersault with the one-and-a-half twist. The Division I dive. And I hadn't killed myself.

———— ∎ ————

There is this wonderful moment when you pull off a dive like this in a competition. It's the three seconds while you're still underwater and you know you've aced it and you can hear all the people cheering but the sound is muffled through the water. It's like hearing this tornado or something in the distance and when you emerge out of the water you suddenly come into the world where the cheering is, and it just takes your breath away. I climbed up the ladder and looked into the stands and everybody was standing up and cheering for me. Then the judges posted their scores: 9.9/9.7/9.9/9.8/10.0.

It was the highest score I'd ever gotten. Suddenly, without any warning, I was a hero. I didn't even get in trouble for not doing the dive I was supposed to do.

We still lost the meet.

We lost because right after I did my dive Lamar Jameson got up and did the exact same dive.

I just sat there on the bench, hanging my head. I think I knew what he was going to do while he was still climbing the ladder to the high dive. When he got to the top, he looked me in the eye, and then he turned around and got into position.

Now I have to say that Lamar's dive wasn't as good as mine. The judges gave him 9.5, 9.5, 9.6, 9.8, and 10.0. The fact that that last judge seemed to be handing out 10s to pretty much anybody took some of the shine off the one he'd given me. Lamar's head wasn't tucked in all the way on the way down, which is the main reason they docked him the points. Still, it was a beautiful dive, and it was all the more impressive that he just got up there and matched me move for move. I had a feeling I'd be competing against Lamar Jameson again soon.

Lamar's dive was enough to ensure Ely winning, but that didn't really make any difference to me. What mattered was that I'd pulled off the dive without even practicing it, and that I'd done something pretty cool while my family and Posie were there, watching. When I got up to head into the lockers with the rest of the team, I looked up in the stands, and there was Thorne, sitting in the back row. He was sitting next to Cecily LaChoy. They had their arms around each other, and they were both wearing T-shirts that said LEMON. Cecily looked like she was the happiest girl in the whole world. Thorne gave me the thumbs-up sign.

When I got outside a little later, Posie was waiting for me. She gave me this big hug. And I realized as I hugged her that for the first time I really wasn't thinking about Sophie anymore. I was thinking about tomorrow, Thanksgiving, and Posie and me, together at last.

On the way home I pulled over at the drugstore and bought more condoms just for the hell of it.

When I got home, the VW Beetle was parked in front of the house again.

I know who it belongs to now. It doesn't belong to Thorne, although it's the same color as Thorne's. No, this Beetle belongs to someone else: Mr. Bond, the senior class homeroom teacher.

Hello??

When I walked in the door he was sitting on the couch with his arm around Mom. The two of them were watching TV and they looked up at me, totally unconcerned, all smiles.

"Hi, Jonah!" said Mom.

"Hi, Jonah!" said Mr. Bond.

"Hi, Mom. Hi, Mr. Bond." I felt like all the blood was draining out of my body. I couldn't believe it. Mr. Bond is Mom's boyfriend, of all people.

Mr. Bond smiled at me. "Oh, you can call me Robere." He said it like it was this French name that rhymes with Pierre. I have to say it's the dumbest name I've ever heard.

Honey came in at that moment, and looked at

Mom and Mr. Bond. "So, Mom. This your new boyfriend?" she said.

"Well, yes. I hope you'll be nice!" Mom said, and laughed nervously.

Honey looked like she was thinking it over. "I don't think so," she said, and left.

"Robere and I have been dating for over a month now," said Mom.

"She's a pretty special lady," said Mr. Bond.

I just stood there, amazed.

"Good job at the meet today," said Mr. Bond. "You're quite an athlete."

"Oh, yes, you were wonderful, Jonah!" said Mom. She stood up suddenly and threw her arms around me, and hugged me hard. "I'm so proud of you. You're doing a great job!" Then she went back to the couch and put her arms around Mr. Bond again and relaxed.

I don't know. Sitting on the couch like that, the two of them kind of looked like teenagers to me. And something in me softened to them. I guess it's fine that Mom has someone in her life. I just wish it wasn't Mr. Bond. It's too weird. I'm already thinking about how awkward it will be when I'm in his homeroom next year.

"Robere is staying overnight tonight," said Mom. "He's going to help make the turkey tomorrow."

"That's appropriate!" shouted Honey from the next room.

"I have a special recipe," Mr. Bond said. "I marinate the turkey in Cointreau."

"What's Cointreau?" I said.

"Oh, it's an orange liqueur," Mr. Bond said, winking at me.

"Ah," I said.

"Robere is going to be around quite a lot from now on," said Mom.

"Oh?" I asked. "Is Mr. Bond moving in with us?"

Mom and Mr. Bond looked at each other and giggled. "We'll see," Mom said.

I went to my room and lay down on the bed. Sometimes I can't believe my own life. It's like this chain of totally bizarre events. I picked up the phone because I was sort of in the mood to talk to someone. First I tried Posie, but Mrs. Hoff said she was out surfing. Then I called Thorne, but there was no answer at his house, and I realized he was probably out on his dad's boat. So I put the phone back in the cradle and I thought about going on the Web, but the idea of encountering Northgirl again would probably drive me crazy wondering who she is, so I just put on some music. It was a while before I realized that the idea of calling Sophie hadn't even occurred to me.

I think I'm over her at last.

Nov. 22, Thanksgiving, 6 P.M.

There's a song that we used to sing on Thanksgiving when we were kids, about It's a gift to be simple, it's a gift to be free. I never used to think about it, at least not about how things being simple is actually a gift, because I always used to kind of take simplicity for granted. But I think it's fair to say I don't do that anymore. Now I wish that things could be more simple. That would definitely be a gift.

I guess you could say a couple of weird things happened on Thanksgiving.

First of all, the morning and early afternoon were pretty nice. I got up and drank coffee with Honey and the two of us watched the Macy's Thanksgiving Day parade on television and it was sort of like we were kids again. I couldn't remember the last time Honey and I just sat around watching television together. I thought about the fact that she was going to Harvard at the end of this summer and that this was probably one of the last times we'd all sit around like this on a Thanksgiving morning. I thought about some of the funny conversations we'd had recently and I had this real swell of emotion for her. But I knew better than to say anything to her about it, because Honey would punch me in the stomach. Still, it was nice.

Posie came over for Thanksgiving dinner, which was nice, although she wasn't very hungry because she'd already had Thanksgiving dinner earlier with her grandparents and her little sister, Caitlin. But she came over anyway because I'd asked her to, and it was pretty great having her sit there as part of our family.

Thorne and his mom and dad were there, too. The three of them looked tired and hungry, which was fine because there was tons of food. It was a little weird seeing Mrs. Wood again, though. She looked thin, and a lot older than I remembered. And Thorne's dad smelled like fish.

Mr. Bond came into the living room wearing an apron and holding this bottle of liqueur. "A little Cointreau, anyone?"

My mom followed him out of the kitchen, and

Mr. Bond put his arm around her and gave her a squeeze.

Thorne's eyes looked like they were going to pop.

"Thorne, you know Mr. Bond," I said.

Thorne smiled. "Yeah, from school."

"Hi, Judith," said Thorne's dad.

"Hi, Sam. Alice," said Mom. "Please, make yourselves at home. This is Robere."

"Robere," said Mrs. Wood. "Now that's a name you don't hear much."

And Mr. Bond said, "It's French."

Honey came in and looked at Mr. Bond and the Woods. She rolled her eyes and said, "Good night, nurse!" and then she left the room.

Mr. Bond frowned, and Mom flapped her hands and said, "Oh, she's a character!"

Then we all sat down in the living room.

Posie started to say, "Mr. Bond, can I get you a—"

"Robere!" Mr. Bond said.

"Robere, can I get you something? A glass of wine?" Posie offered.

"I think I'll have an Irish whiskey," he said.

Posie thought about this for a second.

"Posie, there's a bottle of Bushmills in the cupboard," Mom said.

Posie went to get Mr. Bond an Irish whiskey, and Mom said, "My ex-husband used to drink Bushmills," as if this was a fact that Mr. Bond really wanted to know.

"Bushmills is the Protestant whiskey," Mr. Bond told us. We all nodded like this was something *we* wanted to know. Then he added, "Jameson's is the Catholic whiskey."

And Mom said, "I think whiskey should be free to be liquid!"

Mr. Bond looked kind of sad. "Wouldn't it be nice if we lived in a world where that was true," he said.

Then Posie came out with the Bushmills and gave it to Mr. Bond, and Mom said, "You know, Posie, I think I'll have a Bushmills, too. On the rocks, with a little water?"

I wasn't sure how I felt about Posie being ordered around like she was a waitress, but I sort of liked it that Mom considered her part of the family.

"So how do you know Mr. Bond, Mrs. Black?" Thorne said.

"Robere!" Mr. Bond said.

"Robere. How do you know him?" Thorne asked.

"Would you believe Robere and I went to high school together? Back in Ohio? Then he heard me on the radio, on the very first edition of *Pillow Talk*!" Mom said, beaming with delight.

"Uh-huh," Thorne said.

"He called me up the next day. Didn't you, Robere?"

"I sure did," Mr. Bond said.

"We couldn't believe after all this time we'd both settled down in Pompano!" Mom exclaimed. "It's such a small world."

"You knew each other in high school?" I said. I couldn't believe it.

"Oh, I should say so!" said Mom. And then she actually blushed. This is a woman who talks about sex on the radio. Mom doesn't blush easily.

"Your mother and I dated," said Mr. Bond, with a kind of dreamy expression.

"I dumped him for your father! Can you believe it?" Mom said.

"Sure, I can see that," I said. I didn't mean to be rude or anything. It was just that if I had to choose between Dad and Mr. Bond, I'd definitely go for Dad.

Mom and Mr. Bond started holding hands. "We're making up for lost time," she said.

Honey came in at that moment with a huge plate of cheese. It was the kind of cheese with blue veins in it. She held the plate out to Mr. Bond and Mom.

"Have some stinky cheese, you lovebirds," she said. As she leaned over with the cheese plate, one of her breasts practically fell out of the black scoop-neck top she was wearing.

"Honey, fix yourself," said Mom.

Honey looked at Mom like she was speaking a foreign language. Mr. Bond started cutting into the stinky cheese. Mom made a gesture with her hands, indicating that Honey should pull her shirt up, and Honey rolled her eyes.

"Fix myself? Jeez, Mom, you make it sound like I'm broken."

"I didn't say you were broken," Mom said sweetly.

But Honey was off on a tear. It was weird because I hadn't seen this coming at all. She really laid it into Mom.

"You didn't have to say it! I know what you think!" Honey screamed.

"Honey, what I think I hear you saying is . . ." Mom stammered, trying like hell to behave like patient Dr. Judith.

"Oh, shut up, Mom! Just once, would you shut up?" Honey yelled.

And then she stomped into her room and slammed the door.

Mom looked after her, clearly embarrassed. Finally she said to Robere, "I think she's working out some issues."

"Boys and girls," sighed Mrs. Wood.

Thorne smiled. "Tell me about it," he said.

Finally the turkey was done, and we all sat around the dining room table. Honey didn't come out of her room, and Mom decided not to make her.

I was kind of sad about this, since this was the last Thanksgiving we'd all be together. Still, I was enjoying the meal. I have to say I really love Thanksgiving. I could eat turkey and stuffing and gravy all day. And I felt like I'd finally come to a place of peace, after all the crises of my last year. I know it's totally stupid and corny, but it's true. I had lots of things to be grateful for.

I looked at Posie across the table. She was eating mashed sweet potatoes off her fork, and one strand of her hair was falling down from where she'd tied it up on top of her head. The one piece of hanging hair was coming dangerously close to her sweet potatoes. She was the most beautiful thing I'd ever seen.

Then the phone rang and Honey picked it up. A few seconds later she came in and said, "Jonah, it's for you." And I said, "Excuse me," and got up. Honey stayed where she was, and as I went down the hall to get the phone, she sat down in my chair. I heard her say, "May I have some turkey, please?"

And my mother said, "Of course, dear."

I picked up the phone and I could tell by the static it was long distance.

"Hello? Jonah? Jonah Black?" a girl's voice said.

"Yes," I said. "It's me."

"It's Sophie. Sophie O'Brien. From Masthead?"

The second I heard her voice it was like I'd been blown out of a space capsule and I was floating around the moon. All the feelings I'd ever had for her rushed to the surface again, like water bursting through floodgates. That funny Maine accent. Those sad eyes.

"I don't know if you remember me, but I needed to talk to you." She pronounced it *re-mem-bah*.

"I remember you," I said. "Of course I remember you."

"I guess I owe you some thanks," she said. She sounded nervous. "I guess I owe you more than some thanks."

"For what?" I said.

"For what you did for me last spring."

"What I did? What did I do?" I said. My legs felt loose and I leaned against the wall for balance.

"Oh, you don't have to pretend like it's a secret," she said. "I found out the truth. I feel so stupid. You saved me. I can't believe what you did."

"How did you find out?" I said.

"A friend of yours called me. Thorne Wood? He said you didn't want anyone to know what you did, but he thought I should know. He was right," she said.

"Thorne? Thorne called you and told you the story?" My heart was beating wildly in my chest. I couldn't believe I was talking to Sophie on the phone.

"Yeah," she said. "You're lucky to have a friend like him. I wish I had someone like that." She paused for a second. "I mean, I guess I do have a friend like that. Only I haven't known it. Why did you do it, Jonah? I mean, we hardly knew each other."

"I don't know why I did it," I told her. "It seemed like the right thing to do."

"Thorne told me it's because you're in love with me," Sophie said. "Is that true?"

There was a long pause. I tried to think of the right answer. I had this sudden feeling that whatever I said to her right now was going to determine the course of the rest of my life.

"I was," I said. "I was in love with you."

"But are you now? Are you in love with me now?" Sophie said. Her voice sounded desperate.

"I don't know," I said. "Like you said, we don't really know each other."

There was another long pause.

"I was kind of screwed up last spring," Sophie said. "I was in real trouble."

———— ∎ ————

"I know," I said, although I didn't really know.

"I think I'm better now," she said.

"I'm glad," I said.

"You know, I think I might be in love with you, too," said Sophie. She sounded afraid.

"You are?" I gasped.

"I mean, I don't know. Maybe I'm in love with the idea of you. With the idea of some guy who'd give up everything to get me out of trouble," she said quietly.

I thought about this. I liked the idea of her being in love with the idea of me.

"But is that love?" I asked. "Being in love with the *idea* of somebody? It's not the same as reality, as really being with them."

"I know. That's why I feel so stupid," Sophie said.

"You're not stupid," I said. "I know exactly what you mean."

Both of us were silent for what seemed like a long time. I heard the static on the line. I thought about all the wires that connected my phone to hers, from Florida all the way to wherever she was calling from.

"Where are you now? Are you in Maine?" I asked her.

"Yeah. I'm at my family's in Kennebunkport for Thanksgiving."

"Maine. I've never been to Maine," I said.

"Well, I've never been to Florida," she said. "But I'm coming down over Christmas break. Next month. My father's taking us all to Orlando. Is that far from Pompano Beach?"

"It's not very close," I said.

"But could I drive from there? I mean, it's possible, right?" she said.

"It's possible," I said. I felt sort of seasick at the thought of Sophie driving to Pompano to visit me.

"Jonah, I can't believe I'm sounding like such an idiot. What I want to say is, I want to see you. I want to meet you. Next month when I come to Florida. I want us to be together. Can we do that?" Sophie said.

"Okay," I said without thinking about it at all.

From the next room I heard Posie laugh. Her laughter sounded like sweet, faraway music. Then I heard Sophie's voice in my mind. *Togethah.*

"I'm so happy!" said Sophie. "I'll call you when I know our plans, okay? I'm really looking forward to seeing you. You're . . . you're an amazing person, Jonah Black. But I guess you know that."

"You're pretty amazing, too, Sophie," I said. I couldn't believe what I was saying. I mean I'd wanted to tell her that very thing for like, two years.

"Okay. I gotta go. Love you. 'Bye."

"'Bye," I said, and I hung up. I stood there next to the phone for a few minutes with the sound of her voice in my head. *Love you*, she'd said.

Sophie was coming to Florida. She said she loved me. She said she wanted us to be together. And I'd thought she was gone for good.

Only five minutes before she'd called I was sitting with my family—and Robere—thinking about how grateful I was for this great life, and imagining what was going to happen later on tonight, when Posie and I finally sleep together. And then, out of the blue, everything had changed.

I walked back into the dining room, and everybody looked up. Honey raised her wineglass. "Hey, everybody," she said. "I want to propose a toast!"

"A toast!" said Mr. Bond.

"A toast," my mother echoed, a little nervously. I think she was afraid Honey was going to whip her shirt off or something.

"I want to propose a toast to my big brother, Jonah," Honey said.

"To Jonah!" Thorne and Posie cheered.

I wanted to sit down but I couldn't. Honey was in my chair.

"Hero of the High Dive," Honey said. "Prince of the Eleventh Grade! King of Don Shula High! Jonah Black, Teenage Stud!"

Everyone laughed and drank their wine.

"We are very proud of you, Jonah," said my mother.

"Yes, we're very proud of you," Honey said. "Bonehead."

"Jonah," said Posie, taking my hand. "Who was that on the phone?"

—■—

WILL JONAH AND POSIE EVER GO ALL THE WAY?
WILL NORTHGIRL999 EVER REVEAL HERSELF?
WILL JOHAH EVER TALK TO SOPHIE AGAIN?

FIND OUT IN THE NEXT INSTALLMENT OF
JONAH BLACK'S JOURNAL . . .

The Black Book
[DIARY OF A TEENAGE STUD]

VOL. III: RUN, JONAH, RUN

—■—